THE TEXAS TATTLER

All the news that's barely fit to print!

Fortunes Host "Members-Only" Party

In the wake of Miranda Fortune's shocking revelation about bearing twins out of wedlock comes the next revelation. Notorious bad boy Cameron Fortune fathered *three* illegitimate heirs with *three* different women prior to his death. Family patriarch Ryan Fortune hosted a party at the Double Crown Ranch this past week to welcome these stunned individuals into the family fold.

No expense was spared as the Fortunes served the finest champagne and fanciest hors d'oeuvres. Although one heir declined the invitation, international importer Jonas Goodfellow, Marine Gunnery Sergeant Sam "Storm" Pearce, businessman Justin Bond and a very pregnant Emma Michaels mingled with their new relatives.

"There was something mysterious about Emma," according to one unnamed source. "She didn't want to have much to do with the Fortunes." Of course, this reporter couldn't help noticing that she spent an awful lot of time talking to the P.I. who'd tracked her down. Was she just expressing her gratitude...or could something be brewing between them?

Dear Reader,

Welcome to the world of Silhouette Desire, where you can indulge yourself every month with romances that can only be described as passionate, powerful and provocative!

The ever-fabulous Ann Major offers a *Cowboy Fantasy,* July's MAN OF THE MONTH. Will a fateful reunion between a Texas cowboy and his ex-flame rekindle their fiery passion? In *Cherokee,* Sheri WhiteFeather writes a compelling story about a Native American hero who, while searching for his Cherokee heritage, falls in love with a heroine who has turned away from hers.

The popular miniseries BACHELOR BATTALION by Maureen Child marches on with *His Baby!*—a marine hero returns from an assignment to discover he's a father. The tantalizing Desire miniseries FORTUNES OF TEXAS: THE LOST HEIRS continues with *The Pregnant Heiress* by Eileen Wilks, whose pregnant heroine falls in love with the investigator protecting her from a stalker.

Alexandra Sellers has written an enchanting trilogy, SONS OF THE DESERT: THE SULTANS, launching this month with *The Sultan's Heir.* A prince must watch over the secret child heir to the kingdom along with the child's beautiful mother. And don't miss Bronwyn Jameson's Desire debut—an intriguing tale involving a self-made man who's *In Bed with the Boss's Daughter.*

Treat yourself to all six of these heart-melting tales of Desire—and see inside for details on how to enter our Silhouette Makes You a Star contest.

Enjoy!

Joan Marlow Golan

Joan Marlow Golan
Senior Editor, Silhouette Desire

Please address questions and book requests to:
Silhouette Reader Service
U.S.: 3010 Walden Ave., P.O. Box 1325, Buffalo, NY 14269
Canadian: P.O. Box 609, Fort Erie, Ont. L2A 5X3

The Pregnant Heiress
EILEEN WILKS

Published by Silhouette Books

America's Publisher of Contemporary Romance

Special thanks and acknowledgment are given
to Eileen Wilks for her contribution to
the FORTUNES OF TEXAS: THE LOST HEIRS series.

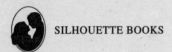

SILHOUETTE BOOKS

ISBN 0-373-76378-6

THE PREGNANT HEIRESS

Copyright © 2001 by Harlequin Books S.A.

Visit Silhouette at www.eHarlequin.com

Printed in U.S.A.

Books by Eileen Wilks

Silhouette Desire

The Loner and the Lady #1008
The Wrong Wife #1065
Cowboys Do It Best #1109
Just a Little Bit Pregnant #1134
Just a Little Bit Married? #1188
Proposition: Marriage #1239
The Pregnant Heiress #1378

Silhouette Intimate Moments

The Virgin and the Outlaw #857
Midnight Cinderella #921
Midnight Promises #982
Night of No Return #1028

EILEEN WILKS

is a fifth-generation Texan. Her great-great-grandmother came to Texas in a covered wagon shortly after the end of the Civil War—excuse us, the War Between the States. But she's not a full-blooded Texan. Right after another war, her Texan father fell for a Yankee woman. This obviously mismatched pair proceeded to travel to nine cities in three countries in the first twenty years of their marriage, raising two kids and innumerable dogs and cats along the way. For the next twenty years they stayed put, back home in Texas again—and still together.

Eileen figures her professional career matches her nomadic upbringing, since she's tried everything from drafting to a brief stint as a ranch hand—raising two children and any number of cats and dogs along the way. Not until she started writing did she "stay put," because that's when she knew she'd come home. Readers can write to her at P.O. Box 4612, Midland, TX 79704-4612.

 Meet the Fortunes of Texas

Meet the Fortunes of Texas's Lost Heirs. Membership in this Texas family has its privileges and its price. As the family gathers to welcome its newest members, it discovers a murderer in its midst...and passionate new romances that only a true-bred Texas love can bring!

CAST OF CHARACTERS

Flynn Sinclair: Although this hardened private investigator's job ended as soon as he'd brought Miranda Fortune's twins to Texas, one look at a very pregnant, scared Emma Michaels told him that his work had only begun....

Emma Michaels: She'd fled from an abusive relationship in the dead of night, but seven months pregnant, this reluctant heiress wasn't quite so fleet-footed. The only person who could help her was a darkly handsome stranger whose deep voice had already inspired a fantasy—or two.

Justin Bond: Getting to know the Fortunes had changed Emma's twin brother...and the first thing on this businessman's "to do" list was wooing back his wife!

Prologue

February: just off I-10, north of Huachuca City, Arizona

She smiled a lot. Flynn couldn't figure out why. The elderly couple she was waiting on now could have been excused for thinking she'd shown up at the truck stop this morning just for the pleasure of looking at the photos the old woman had spread out on the table.

Her smile was bright and natural, too, not forced. Sunnyside up, like the eggs she'd set in front of Flynn a few minutes ago. It made people smile back. Flynn couldn't make sense of that smile.

If the old couple had been paying attention, they would have seen that she didn't have time to stop and ooh over pictures of their grandkids. They would have seen the exhausted smudges beneath those baby-blue eyes, too.

Flynn paid attention. To everything. It was his job.

She detached herself from her elderly admirers and was making her way along the row of booths in her station when a trucker with a handlebar mustache slid out of a booth and stood, blocking her. He tried out a smile that looked creaky from disuse. He also tried to pat her fanny.

She dodged his hand and said something Flynn couldn't catch over the noise in the truck stop. He frowned. The trucker might be a slug or just an idiot. There were plenty of both around, men who would want a taste of that sunshine and grab for it.

He had an urge to explain manners to Handlebar Mustache in terms the man would understand. His fingers twitched with the need to make a fist. But he wasn't needed. Handlebar headed for the register, the lines of his face drooping in disappointment. Flynn's gaze switched to his subject as she hurried behind the counter to replace the coffeepot on its warmer.

She was too skinny. With her brown hair pulled back in that bobbing ponytail she looked like a kid, her face all eyes and smiling mouth, her arms and legs in perpetual motion. In spite of the telltale bulge her stomach made beneath her faded pink uniform, she looked like she ought to be climbing trees and contemplating the mysteries of puberty. Not dealing with its most noticeable result.

She wasn't a child, though. Flynn knew her age to the day. Emma Michaels was thirty-two, single, and until recently she'd lived in San Diego, California. He knew her birthplace, the name of her high school English teacher, her last three places of residence and her mother's name.

Which was more than she knew.

Flynn smiled. He hadn't expected to enjoy this job. His client was a worm, and when you worked for worms you usually found yourself mucking around in dirt. Moreover, he was certain Lloyd Carter had lied to him.

By itself, that wouldn't have bothered him much. Clients

lied. Everyone lied. He was often amazed at the amount of trouble people would take to cover up some piddly little sin that didn't amount to a hill of beans to anyone but themselves. Lying was a skill that came packaged with language, and in Flynn's line of work, spotting those lies was a necessary talent.

Lloyd Carter was a good liar, but not good enough. Nothing put Flynn on his guard faster than someone who insisted he was being totally honest. Flynn was doing well enough these days that he didn't have to work for a worm if the job didn't interest him. Even though Carter claimed that Miranda Fortune wanted him to contact the twins, Carter's explanations and candid gray eyes had failed to impress him.

In spite of that, he'd taken the job. There was a debt involved, a matter of family and honor. Death didn't cancel a debt, not to Flynn's way of thinking, and the people Carter had wanted him to find were Fortunes. Not that they knew it.

He'd made the worm cough up a big retainer before taking the case. He would have worked for free if one of the Fortune family had been his client, but there was no point in letting Carter off the hook, and Carter's credit was bad.

Flynn sipped from the chipped cup and grimaced. The coffee tasted like it had been brewed about the time the cracked vinyl in the seat he sat on was new. He'd had worse, and been in worse places than this. Part of the hazards of his trade. But he hadn't had much worse.

He drank it anyway. He needed a reason to linger until things slowed down enough for him to speak to Emma Michaels about the family she didn't know she had.

Watching her was surprisingly pleasant. She was too thin, she smiled too much, she was pregnant—the woman had strings and obligations sticking out all over her, like porcupine quills. She was a flake, too. When she'd brought him his eggs he'd commented on the colored stones in her bracelet. She'd told him cheerily that there was a stone for each of her chakras. The bracelet was supposed to balance her energy, or some crap like that.

No, God knew he wasn't interested in her personally. He just liked looking at her. She had all the charm of a friendly kitten. She also had very nice legs. World-class legs.

The protectiveness he felt didn't surprise him. Habit died hard, and in spite of that smile, she looked like a waif in need of help.

The stir of masculine interest did.

She bustled around behind the counter, loading her tray with plates of pancakes, eggs, biscuits and toast. Flynn found himself watching the quick twitch of her hips as she hurried past him to a booth in the corner. She wore a pale-pink uniform reminiscent of the fifties with a pair of up-to-the-minute athletic shoes...and her stomach pulled the uniform tight enough to make the rear view appealing. She had a great ass to go with those excellent legs.

Flynn frowned. He wasn't supposed to be appreciating his subject's ass.

He watched her deal with the truckers and wondered how someone as guileless as Emma Michaels survived in this world. She didn't look like she would be able to lie worth spit.

Yet she *was* lying. Flynn's curiosity itched strongly about that. Emma Michaels was calling herself Emma Jackson now, which had made tracking her difficult. Being pregnant and unwed might account for the lie—shoot, just working as a waitress in this place was reason enough to invent a husband. Only why change her name? He'd checked her finger when she waited on him. She hadn't bought a ring to back up the pretense.

Chances were, her reason for using a fake name had nothing to do with his case, so that, technically, it was none of his business. But once Flynn's curiosity was aroused, it was hard to ignore. He wanted to know why such a lousy liar was trying to pull off such a big lie.

Maybe, he thought as he took another sip of his coffee, she would tell him. She might be willing to explain it once he gave her the good news. He was looking forward to that. It wasn't every day he got to tell a down-on-her-luck young woman with a baby on the way that she was going to be rich.

By nine forty-five, business at the truck stop had thinned out. The other waitress, a heavyset woman with big hair, was refilling the sugar and salt and pepper shakers in her station, and Emma was headed his way with the coffeepot.

Flynn decided it was time. He felt a tingle of anticipation. Would she be more excited about the money, or learning who her mother was?

Even good news could be a shock. He would try to break it to her gently, but he hoped she was tougher than she looked. He wasn't much good at tact and sensitivity. His sisters had mentioned that he had all the emotional subtlety of a sledgehammer.

Emma Jackson-Michaels stopped at his table, coffeepot in hand, but didn't fill his cup. "We have some nice teas, too," she said brightly.

He looked at her blankly. "Teas?"

When she nodded, her ponytail bounced. "Too much caffeine is hard on your system."

"I like coffee."

"If you say so, but I can't help noticing that you look a little tense. You might try some of the chamomile. It's good for relaxing. There's some for sale up at the cash register."

"This doesn't look like the sort of place that would sell herbal teas."

"It was my suggestion." Her voice didn't go with the kitten image. It was low, almost husky—a satin-sheet kind of voice, the sort of voice a man imagined whispering in his ear late at night. "Henry is a little resistant to new ideas. I'm trying to talk him into offering a vegetable plate, but he thinks a meal has to include some portion of a dead animal."

His mouth quirked up. "I guess I have something in common with Henry, then."

"A lot of people do." She looked disappointed but still cheerful as she relented and poured a stream of sludge into his cup. "Are you waiting for someone?"

"Yeah." Up close, she didn't look quite so young, though she could have passed for twenty-five easier than thirty-two. There were tiny creases at the corners of her eyes from all that smiling. Her cheeks were plump, unlike the rest of her, and she had cute eyebrows. They were thin and shaped into curves of mild astonishment above those big eyes. "Do you pluck your eyebrows?"

"What?"

Why had he asked her that? Annoyed, Flynn pushed his cup away. "Never mind. I need to talk to you."

Wariness slid across her blue eyes, but she kept smiling. "My boss wouldn't like that, I'm afraid. Henry has this idea we're supposed to wait on several customers, not just one."

"I'm not trying to pick you up. Here." He raised up slightly so he could dig into his back pocket for his wallet, which held his ID. "My name's Flynn Sinclair. I'm a P.I., and you—"

"I have to go," she said abruptly.

That wasn't wariness he saw in her eyes now. It was fear. Real fear. She edged away.

He grabbed her wrist. It was so narrow his fingers overlapped, which made him feel large and clumsy. "Hey, don't worry. I have good news for you." He gave her his best trust-me smile. "It's about your mother."

"Oh." She smiled wider than ever, but it was neither real nor natural now. "My mother. Of course. I'd love to talk to you about my mother, but I can't stop to chat when I'm working. You understand. If you don't mind waiting until my shift is over, we can talk then, okay?"

A truly lousy liar, he thought, letting go of her wrist. "Sure, no problem. I'll wait here for you."

"That's great." She spoke brightly. Her knuckles were white where she gripped the coffeepot. "I'm looking forward to it. I haven't heard from—Mom—in awhile."

Flynn watched as his subject fled for the kitchen. His curiosity was itching fit to kill. She was going to bolt. He didn't know why, but he knew she was going to bolt.

The back door, he thought, rising and pulling a couple bills out of his wallet. Every restaurant had a delivery entrance off the kitchen. She'd slip out that way, thinking he was waiting patiently for her out here.

Flynn was a big man, but he could move quickly when he wanted. He tossed the bills at the cashier and was out the door before the woman had done more than blink at him.

The air was sharp and dry despite the light dusting of snow on the parking lot and the yucca, creosote and dirt that surrounded it. Flynn spared a brief thought for the jacket he'd left in his car, then forgot the temperature as he reached the rear of the truck stop. A strip of pavement containing Dumpsters, employees' cars, a tottering stack of empty crates and a stray cat separated the building from the land.

There was no sign of Emma. But Flynn knew which car was hers—the aging red Ford Escort on the other side of a jacked-up pickup that looked ready to compete in a monster truck pull.

Her car was still here, so she hadn't run. Yet. Flynn jogged over to it, then stood there shaking his head. The paint was peeling, making the Ford look as if it had leprosy. How had she made it here from San Diego in this heap?

Desperation or stupidity, he thought, bending to pet the stray cat, which was twining itself madly around his legs. Maybe both.

He heard the door to the kitchen slam and the sound of running feet—soft footfalls, like a skinny, slightly pregnant woman in athletic shoes might make. He abandoned his feline admirer and straightened just as she rounded the side of the oversize pickup.

She saw him, stopped dead and shrieked.

"I didn't mean to startle you," he said quickly, holding his hands out, palms up, and trying to look harmless. Unfortunately, he wasn't any better at harmless than he was at sensitivity. "I just need to talk to you for a minute. I was hired to find you—"

"I know," she said, her voice soft and breathless. "But please, please—tell him you couldn't find me. He—he's crazy. You don't know what he'll do. Or at least give me time to leave town. You could do that, couldn't you?"

She knew? His brows drew together. According to Carter, she knew nothing about her family. "I can't lie to a client." Not much, anyway. "Anyway, he already knows where you are."

"Oh, God," she whispered, and shivered.

He frowned. "Don't you have a jacket? It's too cold out here for a little thing like you."

The back door slammed again. The footfalls Flynn heard this time were heavy, solid. He grimaced.

"Emma?" The voice was heavy, too. Deep and heavy and obviously male. "Are you okay? Where are you?"

"Back here, Henry!"

Harmless, Flynn reminded himself. Think harmless. He smiled harmlessly at her. "I'm not here to make trouble for you. I want to tell you about your mother. Your family.''

For the first time, anger flashed in her eyes. ''I don't have any family. I sure don't have a mother.''

''No, she—''

''You get away from her!''

Emma's protector had arrived. Not many men were bigger than Flynn, but this one was. He wore a huge, stained apron wrapped around the middle of his three-hundred plus pounds, and brandished a butcher knife the size of a small sword. His face had been badly scarred by acne thirty or more years ago, a condition that the grizzled stubble on his cheeks didn't quite cover.

''Don't get your panties in a wad,'' Flynn said, irritated. ''I'm not going to hurt her. I'm a private investigator. If you promise not to get excited, I'll get my license out and prove it.''

The big man took a threatening step forward. The hard desert sunlight gleamed on the steel of his knife. ''What d'you mean, excited? You calling me names?''

Flynn sighed. Some days, nothing went right.

''Henry.'' His subject put her hand on the man's arm. ''It's all right.''

''All right? You get so scared you quit, you don't even give notice, you go tearing out of my place like the devil was on your heels, you say it's all right? You!'' He scowled at Flynn. ''I dunno anything about licenses or private investigators. I know you scared Emma. You go away. Now.''

''Listen,'' Flynn said to Emma, abandoning the effort to look harmless and settling for determined. He was better at that. ''Give me five minutes. If you don't like what I have to tell you, you can go back to work, or peel out of here in your car—assuming it's running—or whatever. Five minutes.'' He glanced at her mountainous protector. ''Alone.''

''No way.'' Henry waved his knife.

Emma patted the man on one huge arm. She looked distracted and painfully unsure with those curvy eyebrows of hers trying to frown and managing only to make her look like a perplexed kitten.

She was so damned cute. ''Okay, okay,'' Flynn said. ''This isn't strictly ethical, but I'll make you a deal. If, after I talk to you, you're still worried about my client knowing where you are, I'll give you eight hours' head start.'' And then he'd find her again.

''What did you say your name was again?''

''Flynn. Flynn Sinclair.''

''That's Flynn with two n's?''

''Yeah,'' he said, baffled by her interest in spelling.

She chewed on her lip a moment. ''That makes your heart number a one—very independent. But your personality number is two, so you're kind and, ah, reassuring.'' She looked at him dubiously, obviously doubting the accuracy of her forecast.

Definitely a flake. A pretty one, but a flake. ''That's me. Kind of reassuring.''

She chewed on that unpainted lip. ''I don't think he would send someone to hurt me. That's not his style. And you've seen this man now, Henry, so you could testify if....'' She straightened her shoulders. ''All right. Five minutes. But show me that ID of yours first.''

Not a complete flake, he thought as he dug into his pocket again. Checking his ID was a good idea if she thought he might be tempted to conk her on the head as soon as they were alone. And apparently she did. Damn it, his curiosity was getting tangled up with those blasted protective urges.

Flynn flipped his wallet open and held it out, displaying

his driver's license—with the photo that made him look like he belonged on the Ten Most Wanted list—and his investigator's license. She gave both a careful study, then stepped back so Henry could see them, too.

"You sure this is what you want—to be out here with *him?*" The mountain glared at Flynn.

"He won't go away until I listen to him." She patted a massive arm again. "You'd better get back to the kitchen. Something's probably burning."

Henry lumbered off, muttering that he'd leave the door open, just in case, and she'd better not even think about running off in that uniform and with her station in a mess.

When he was gone, Flynn looked into a pair of wary blue eyes. Poor kitten. How best to start? "Thirty-two years ago, a desperate young woman left two babies in front of the sheriff's office in Dry Creek, Nevada."

Her brows almost managed a real frown this time. "Wait a minute. Two babies?"

"A boy and girl."

"You're not talking about me, then."

Yes, he was. "The young woman's name was Miranda Fortune." He waited, but she didn't react. Maybe she hadn't heard of the Fortunes. They were well-known in Texas, but that was one of the few western states Emma hadn't lived in. "She was only seventeen, dead broke and estranged from her family. Miranda is your mother, Emma. And she wants very badly to meet you."

He wouldn't have thought a face like hers could look stony. But it did. "So you say, but your client is a man, not a woman. You said *he* already knew where I was."

"My client is Lloyd Carter, Miranda's ex-husband."

The rest of her face still wasn't giving much away, but something uncertain moved behind the blue of her eyes. She blinked once, slowly. "My...father?"

"No." He spoke as gently as he could. "Miranda didn't

meet Carter until several months after you were born. I don't know who your father was.''

She swallowed. ''This man—this Carter—are you sure he's who he says he is?''

Flynn had been putting some things together. Emma had gotten pregnant while she was living in San Diego. She'd left town in a big hurry, changed her name and was running scared. Scared of the man who got her pregnant? Afraid of a custody battle—or of the man himself? ''I check out all my clients. Carter's on the slimy side of handsome, but he's definitely who he claims to be.''

She was stiff all over—her shoulders, her back, her expression. ''How old is he? What does he look like?''

''He looks like a two-bit actor—weathered face, lots of smile lines, good cap job on his teeth. Wiry, fairly fit for his age—which is fifty-three, despite what he claims. Dark hair, gray eyes.''

Tension sighed out of her, leaving the slim shoulders slumped. ''That's not Steven.''

''Who's Steven?''

She made a vague gesture. ''Never mind. You say he hired you to find me? Was he acting for his ex-wife?''

''More or less.'' Mostly less, but the situation was complicated. Flynn didn't think this was the time to go into details.

She was looking dazed now. ''So she's alive. I've wondered...but it doesn't really change anything.''

''Of course it does. Maybe your mother didn't do right by you when you were a baby, but she wasn't much more than a child herself then. She's got a bucketful of regrets now, and the money to do something about them. I'm to make whatever arrangements are necessary to get you to come to her for a visit—or to stay, if you like. She's living in Texas now, close to her family.'' He paused. ''Your family, too. The Fortunes.''

"Well..." She didn't think about it long before shaking her head. "No, I don't think so. I don't...this is awfully sudden." Her smile crept out shyly. "She could write to me if she wants, though. You can tell her my address."

Appealing to sentiment hadn't worked. Flynn was conscious of feeling disappointed in her, which was absurd. He switched tactics smoothly. He'd hit her where it counted with most people: the wallet. "One thing I haven't mentioned. The Fortunes are rich. Not your garden variety rich, either. Buying-small-countries rich."

"Oh. Yes, I think I've heard of them," she said vaguely, as if it weren't important. "I don't pay a lot of attention to gossip columns and such."

"Miranda wants to settle some money on you."

That got a reaction, but not the one he expected. Instead of greed lighting a spark in her eyes, impatience made her snappish. "I don't need her money. I do just fine on my own."

He glanced at the car beside them. Three bald tires and peeling paint didn't equal "doing just fine" to him. "Maybe so. But what's fine for you might not be fine for that baby you're expecting."

Her chin tilted up. "I can take care of my baby. And myself. And now," she said, haughty as a duchess, "if you'll excuse me, I'd better get back to work." She turned away.

Yeah, that's one great ass, he thought as she walked away from him and several million dollars. Pretty face, too, in spite of those smudges beneath her eyes, and what a smile she's got. Pity she's a flake.

He had one last thing to try. "Maybe you forgot what I said about there being two babies," he called out. "Are you at all interested in meeting your brother, Emma?"

She stopped and turned slowly to face him. "You're just

saying that to get me to...a brother? I don't...do I really
have a brother?''

She wanted to believe him. She wanted it so badly he
could taste her yearning in the air between them. This was
the reaction he'd expected when he'd told her about her
mother. He walked up to her and said quietly, ''His name
is Justin. He's your twin. I found him, too. Last week I
told him about you and your mother, and he's making arrangements to fly there to meet her. He's expecting to see
you there, too.''

''He's in Texas?''

''He will be, in another day or two.''

''I have a brother. A *twin* brother.'' Wonder filled her
eyes.

''A fraternal twin.'' Amusement lightened his voice.
''Obviously.''

She hugged her arms around herself tightly. ''All right.
I'll go.''

One

April: San Antonio

There were thirteen different lip colors on the dressing table in front of Emma. Four were pencils, three were tubes, four more were in little pots and two of them looked like a kindergartner's crayons. She even had accessories for them: a teensy brush and two sizes of sharpeners.

Emma generally owned one or two lipsticks that she forgot to use. What was she doing with thirteen lip colors that needed their own accessories?

"Emma?" The voice that drifted up the stairs was raised enough to be heard, but fell far short of being a yell. Miranda Fortune never did anything as crude as yelling. "Are you almost ready?"

That's how she'd ended up with thirteen lip colors. Emma sighed. "Almost!"

Which was almost true. She had her dress on. She just

had to do her hair and her makeup and find some shoes, and she'd be ready…ready for a party she didn't want to attend.

Emma grimaced and reached for one of the crayon-type lipsticks. It was appropriate; she felt like a kindergartner playing with makeup as she drew an outline on her lips with a purply-red crayon and then colored it in.

She wasn't exactly dreading the party. She didn't expect to fit in, but she was used to that. And her brother would be there. Two brothers, actually—she had a half brother, too, and a half sister. But it was her twin she thought of. Justin.

She smiled at her reflection, noticed the dimple in her left cheek and smiled wider. Her brother had a smile just like hers, dimple and all. The first time she'd seen him smile she'd laughed in delight. Not that she got to see his smile often—or him, either. This was his second trip to Texas, though, his second trip to see *her*. And Miranda, of course. Justin Bond was a very successful businessman based in Pittsburgh; he was always busy, usually too serious and very private.

But when he did smile, the sun came out. Oh, how she was looking forward to seeing him again!

Flynn Sinclair might be there, too.

Anticipation took on another note, a deeper, less certain chord that resonated in places Emma didn't want to notice.

She heard the light tread on the stairs and tensed. *Stay with your breath,* she told herself, and focused on the slow in and out of her breathing the way the monk at the temple in Taos had taught her.

Her muscles were relaxed again by the time Miranda spoke from the doorway. "Kane and Allison are here to take us to the ranch."

Kane Fortune was Miranda's son from her marriage to Lloyd Carter. He'd taken the Fortune name soon after Miranda moved back to Texas. Emma hadn't felt the immediate connection with Kane she'd experienced with her twin. Mostly she felt wary. "I may have exaggerated about being ready," she said cheerfully without turning around. "But it will only take two shakes to finish up. There's not much that can be done with this mop of mine."

There were two women in Emma's mirror: one with dark, frantically curly hair, one with smooth blond hair swept into a perfect chignon. Miranda Fortune was sleek, blond and lovely, impossibly elegant tonight in diamonds and a long sweep of black silk.

"Oh, my." Emma spun around on the small stool. "Don't you look gorgeous!"

Miranda's lips turned up in a surprised smile. "Thank you. You look wonderful, too. Don't worry about Kane. He won't mind waiting a few minutes."

Emma had her doubts about that, but she kept them to herself.

"Oh, do stand up and let me see how the dress looks!"

Emma's dress was yet another compromise in a long line of compromises she'd made in the eight weeks since she came here. She was holding firm about the important thing, though. She wouldn't let Miranda settle any money on her. A small trust fund for the baby, sure. That was fine. But Emma didn't want to be rich. She didn't know *how* to be rich. Who would she be if she had tons of money she hadn't earned herself? No one she knew.

The dress was pretty, though. Miranda had wanted to take her to one of the expensive shops she patronized; Emma had wanted to go to a factory outlet store she'd discovered. In the end, they'd found this one on the fifty-percent-off rack at an upscale department store. It was more colorful than elegant, which suited Emma.

The layers of tissue-thin gauze swished pleasantly around her ankles when she stood. She grinned and patted her tummy. "I look like a cross between a hippie and a hippo—one of those dancing hippos in *Fantasia,* maybe." And nothing at all like the polished woman standing in front of her.

"You look beautiful."

The words were simply spoken and obviously sincere. Emma flushed. "Well—thank you." A sharp jab from inside made her grin. "Elmo is more excited about this party than I am."

"Elmo?" Both elegant eyebrows rose. "I hope that's a joke. Yesterday you called the baby Abigail."

Emma shrugged. "Elmo, Abigail, Zeke, Penelope—I haven't made up my mind."

Miranda smiled. "It might be easier to decide on a name if you'd let the doctor tell you what its sex is."

"I like surprises."

"That's good, because I've brought you one." She held out a small, silver-wrapped box the size that jewelry came in. Her lips still smiled, but her eyes were uncertain.

Emma felt a now-familiar stab of irritation. "That's very nice of you, Miranda, but you really have to stop *buying* me things all the time. It makes me uncomfortable. You're already giving me an allowance—"

"This isn't anything expensive, truly." She offered the box again. "If you don't like it, you don't have to wear it."

Emma had long since realized that her idea of expensive and Miranda's were vastly different. Reluctantly she held her hand out and summoned a smile. "How can I refuse?"

The box held jewelry, just as Emma had suspected—a necklace with a dainty silver chain. "Oh...how pretty!" She held it up. The pendant was a stylized yin-yang symbol.

"I hoped you would like it. You seem very interested in that sort of thing."

Emma felt touched—and guilty. Miranda was trying so hard, and Emma hated to keep disappointing her. But what Miranda wanted from Emma wasn't possible. "I'll wear it tonight. Would you put it on for me?"

She sat back down at the dressing table. It was a pretty, totally feminine piece of furniture, covered at the moment with the detritus from Emma's attempt at applying makeup. The mirror showed her Miranda's face as the woman moved up behind her.

They looked nothing alike. Their hair was different, their eyes were different, their mouths, the very shape of their faces...but the nose on the older woman's face was a lot like hers. Straight and a little too short.

It should have been a comforting discovery. After years of looking for her features on the faces of strangers, Emma ought to be glad to find her nose on the face of the woman who had given birth to her.

She wasn't.

When Miranda bent to fasten the necklace, her fingers brushed Emma's nape. Feelings rushed in—crowded, confused feelings that made her want rather frantically to get away. She summoned a smile. "I love it."

"Maybe I could fix your hair." Miranda touched one curl lightly. "You'd look lovely in a French braid, and I have a little silver clasp we could use."

Something strong and ugly flashed through Emma. Something she had no intention of acknowledging or encouraging. She took a deep breath and let it out slowly. "Great. I can never do anything with my hair."

It was going to be a long night.

The party was being given by her uncle, Ryan Fortune, at his ranch outside the city in Red Rock, Texas. Emma rode there in the comfort of plush leather seats with classical music throbbing gently from the car speakers.

Miranda didn't speak much once they got in the car, and Kane and Allison spoke mostly to each other. and Emma was glad. Making conversation could be a strain with all those undercurrents swirling around.

There would be undercurrents at the party, too, but not such personal ones. It was a big "welcome to the family" bash for her, Justin, and two other Fortune cousins—Sam "Storm" Pearce and Jonas Goodfellow—that the family had recently discovered, thanks to the efforts of Flynn Sinclair.

That man sure got around. He'd made his way into Emma's thoughts far too often in the past eight weeks.

It was only natural that she would think of him sometimes, she told herself as the lights of San Antonio faded behind them. He'd been the catalyst for some important events in her life. It was no wonder she kept remembering that deep, laconic voice.

Elmo—or maybe Abigail—gave her a hard kick in the ribs in rebuttal.

Okay, so maybe she thought of Flynn a little too often. But there was no harm in a fantasy or two. She wasn't *really* interested in the man, no matter what effect he'd had on her unruly hormones. He was a P.I., for heaven's sake. One step removed from a bounty hunter.

Like Steven.

Emma's shoulders tensed against the rush of fear. She had to stop reacting that way. It had been months since she'd fled San Diego in the dead of night, and Steven was very good at finding people who didn't want to be found. Surely, if he had been determined to track her down, he would have done it by now.

No, she wouldn't think about Steven. He was part of her past, not her present or her future. Better to think about all her new relatives. Fortunately, she'd already met a few of them—like her uncle, Ryan Fortune.

She tasted the phrase in her mind: her uncle, Ryan Fortune. Uncle Ryan. It had an odd ring to it. Odd, but pleasant.

He had come to see her soon after she arrived in San Antonio. There was something very solid about Ryan Fortune, a grounded quality she hadn't expected in a man with his wealth. She liked him. He didn't push. He hadn't so much as raised an eyebrow over her being pregnant and unmarried, either.

She glanced at the woman sitting beside her in the silver Mercedes sedan. Miranda didn't *mean* to push. Whatever she had been like when she was young, back when she ran away from home and gave birth to two babies she didn't keep, she was a nice woman now. A bit too perfect, maybe, but Emma didn't hold that against her. And Miranda was clearly delighted about the baby.

All in all, Emma thought she could like Miranda, too—if only the woman would stop trying to be her mother. It was too late for that. Years and years too late.

Ryan and Lily Fortune's house at the Double Crown Ranch looked like an old-time Spanish hacienda. It was large, lovely and easy to get lost in.

Not that she was really lost, Emma assured herself as she paused at one end of a hallway she was almost sure she'd seen before. Just turned around. She could hear voices, the sound muted by the thick walls of the house into a sort of human ocean, rising and falling in the distance. She must be headed in the right direction.

Of course, she could have asked for directions. She'd stumbled across the kitchen in her wanderings; she should have asked one of the people who'd been clattering pans and dishes. But she hadn't. Instead, she'd hurried off in another direction. It was absurd, but she hadn't wanted to be seen. She felt guilty for having misplaced herself. As if she had no business being here—not here in this house, not here with these people.

Well. She paused and shook her head. It didn't take Sigmund Freud to figure out what *that* meant.

Emma trailed her fingers lightly over the stuccoed wall beside her. Would she ever feel as if she belonged in these grand surroundings? As if these strangers were really family?

Probably not, she thought wistfully. She wasn't good at making permanent connections with people. But…her hand stole to her stomach, her fingers spreading to cup the curve protectively. A tiny knee or elbow butted against her palm as her baby shifted inside her.

Emma might never belong here. But her baby would.

She smiled. Alice—or maybe Edward—would grow up knowing these people, maybe running down this hall when the two of them came for a visit, small, bare feet slapping the tile floor. Emma's child wouldn't even notice the niches in the thick walls that displayed pottery and other art objects, much less think about what they cost. They would all be familiar. As with all familiar things, they would be comfortingly invisible.

But it was foreign to Emma, strange and obtrusive. She remembered the objects better than the people—like the solid oak front door, the huge fireplace. She'd tried to keep track of faces and names, but there were so many of them, an overabundance of strange new relatives.

Not that everyone here was related to her. Some were relatives by marriage, others were friends or neighbors of the family. But there were an awful lot of Fortunes. Some, like her, were Fortunes by birth, but they bore other names. Like her new cousins, "Storm" and Jonas.

They had been fathered by her Uncle Ryan's black-sheep brother, Cameron, who had died several years ago. Emma had yet another new cousin, courtesy of her Uncle Cameron's womanizing, but Holly Douglas wouldn't be at the party tonight. She refused to leave her home in Alaska.

Jonas had brought a bottle of port for their host—no, for Uncle Ryan, she corrected herself mentally. It was a courteous gesture…and one that hadn't occurred to Emma.

She sighed. She didn't know how to act with these people.

The sound of voices was growing louder, reassuring her that she was on her way back. She turned a corner and caught a glimpse of someone vanishing into one of the rooms that opened off the next short stretch of hallway.

She grimaced. Maybe a lot of the names and faces had blurred, but she had no trouble matching that particular brassy blond head to a face and a name. Thank goodness Leeza hadn't seen her. One encounter with Lloyd Carter's current wife had been more than enough. The woman was as sticky-sweet as strawberry jam, with big, bouncy breasts and big, sly eyes shadowed by inch-thick mascara.

Leeza had cornered Emma earlier and made a big deal about how she'd urged her husband to hire Flynn Sinclair to find Emma and Justin. She'd cooed about how her heart had been wrenched to think of "you poor little things" growing up without a mother.

Phooey. That woman had never done anything for anyone unless there was something in it for her.

Emma hurried down the hall, wanting to be somewhere else when Leeza came out of that door. What was the woman doing, anyway? Maybe she was lost. That was the charitable explanation; Leeza must be as much of a stranger to this house as Emma was. Somehow Emma doubted it, though. More likely, she was prying. She was the sort who would make an excuse to use your bathroom so she could peek inside the medicine cabinet, hoping to find some interesting dirt to sling.

Emma had nearly reached the arched entry to the great

room, where people in fancy dress were milling around, talking and laughing and making Emma's head pound.

Oh, Lord. She really didn't want to go back in there. Normally Emma made friends easily. New faces, new places—she was used to both, and good at making herself at home wherever she was. And she genuinely liked people. She considered mingling with strangers an opportunity, not a chore. Normally.

But nothing seemed to be normal anymore.

Well, she wasn't going to hang out in the hallway all night. She took a deep breath and plunged back into the crowd.

She made it three feet before someone stopped her.

"There you are. I've been looking for you."

She knew that voice—deep, rumbly, as if each word rolled up from somewhere deep inside the big, broad chest of the man. She turned, her heartbeat picking up speed. "Flynn. I mean, Mr. Sinclair. I wondered if you would be here tonight. Ryan told me you'd been invited."

He was too big. That was, once again, the first thing she noticed about the man—his size. Emma didn't like oversize men with tough-guy faces. Not even when they had Superman hair, black and shiny as wet Magic Marker, with an unruly curl that parted company with the rest of his hair to make an adorable little squiggle on his forehead.

"Flynn works fine." The corner of his mouth kicked up in the cocky grin she remembered. "I've been hoping I'd see you tonight."

He had? "Well—that's flattering." An elbow jabbing her rib cage from inside made her rub her stomach soothingly, reminding her that he hadn't meant that the way she wanted to take it. He couldn't have, she thought wryly. Not when she was doing her seven-month impression of a blimp. "I was hoping to see you, too. I never thanked you."

His eyebrows lifted slightly. "No thanks needed. I did what I'd been hired to do. But I'm curious. When I, ah, talked to you at the truck stop, I didn't get the impression that gratitude was one of your reactions."

"I was a little spooked at the time," she admitted. No need to tell him that she'd felt uneasy from the moment he'd sat down in her station, long before he'd scared her by telling her he was a P.I. Flynn Sinclair simply did not have a reassuring face. His nose had been broken at least once; his cheeks were sunken, dark with beard shadow, and his eyes were set too deeply beneath thick black eyebrows.

But they were green, those eyes. Not hazel, not even grass-green, but the bright, hard color of an old 7-Up bottle.

And they were laughing at her right now. "I figured that out."

"You probably wondered why."

He shrugged those oversize shoulders. "I figured that out, too. You were running scared of someone—Steven Shaw. The man who got you pregnant."

"I—how did you—did I mention him?"

"Yeah." There wasn't a trace of a smile left on his face now, and his eyes had that hard, unwavering focus that unnerved her and made something inside her tingle. "Are you glad I found you now? And dragged you kicking and screaming into your family?"

"Not kicking and screaming," she protested. "But—yes, I'm glad." Amusement mixed with pleasure. "I've got a brother now. Two of them, actually. Not to mention a half sister, two aunts by marriage, an uncle and more cousins than I've been able to count."

"And a mother."

"Yes, of course."

"Kane says you and Miranda are having problems."

They'd discussed her? She didn't like that.

"Well, he's wrong. Miranda and I get along fine. I'm

afraid Kane and Gabrielle don't entirely approve of me. I guess that's natural—I'm living, breathing proof that their mother isn't quite the perfect person they'd like to think. Kane, especially, is protective of her.''

''Funny. I didn't get the impression that Kane disapproves of you. Maybe you're having trouble warming up to him and Gabrielle because you're jealous of their relationship with Miranda.''

''I don't know Miranda well enough to be jealous of her. Besides, jealousy is a very destructive emotion.''

''I'd call it a very human emotion. If you don't know Miranda well, that's because you never had the chance, while Kane and Gabrielle had her all these years. Stands to reason that you'd be jealous of that.''

''Has anyone ever told you that you are a very annoying man?''

''Once or twice.'' He shrugged. ''I didn't want to see you so we could argue about family relationships, though. I've checked out that boyfriend of yours, and—''

''You've *what?*'' Annoyance boiled over into temper.

''Checked out Steven Shaw. He's bad news.''

''Tell me something I don't know! What right did you have to go digging around in my personal life?''

''I'm a P.I. If I waited until people gave me permission to dig around, I wouldn't get much work done.''

''And were you working?'' she demanded. ''I thought your job ended when you found me!''

''I guess it did, technically. But I got a call a few days ago from a man named Mathers. He said he'd heard I was looking for you. Pretended he had information for me, while he tried to pump me for information.''

The blood drained from her head. ''Richard Mathers is Steven's friend,'' she whispered.

''That's what I discovered when I checked him out. And

that's why I decided to find out more about your old boy-friend.''

"Former fiancé," she corrected absently. Had Flynn's meddling tipped Steven off?

"Whatever." He shook his head. "I should have gone with my itch to start with. Loose ends have a way of snapping back on a man."

"What did you tell Richard?"

"Not a damned thing. You think I'm an idiot, or just unscrupulous?"

"Are you sure? Steven used to say that people don't realize how much they're giving away once he gets them talking. He's...very good at that sort of thing."

His voice turned dry. "I'm not bad at it myself, so I recognize the tricks when someone tries to play them on me. Besides, it wasn't your boyfriend I talked to. It was his buddy, and Mathers isn't all that good."

Her head was spinning with possibilities, each more frightening than the last. "Stop calling Steven my boy-friend. He never was, not really—"

"That baby didn't get started all by itself."

"You know, when you lift one eyebrow that way, your whole face gets sarcastic. You don't even have to change your voice. It's very annoying. What I *meant* was that I object to the word 'boyfriend.' It's so silly and juvenile. Steven and I were engaged."

"You do know how to pick 'em, don't you?"

How could she have entertained even one fleeting fantasy about this man? "I think I'll go talk to someone else for awhile. Someone who will make more of an effort not to insult me."

"Ah—sorry. I didn't mean to—hey, don't walk off. I need to ask you a couple of questions." He wrapped one big hand around her arm.

She jerked her arm away. "I don't like being grabbed."

"Okay, okay. Is Shaw likely to trash my office looking for my case file on you? How fixated is he?"

"I...I don't know." It was a frightening thought. Would Steven be so determined to find her that he would break into Flynn's office to learn where she was? "He might."

"Hmm." His eyes looked very green, very sharp. "Well, I'll make sure he can't learn anything from me, even if he is stupid enough to search my office. Since you're staying with your mother, your name shouldn't be out where he can find it, like on utility bills. Have you used your social security number at all?"

She shook her head. "Steven used to talk to me about how he tracked people down, so I know better than to do that." She tried for a smile, but it wobbled. "Which has made finding a job rather difficult."

"A job?" He drew those thick eyebrows together. "Why in the hell would you be looking for a job? You're seven months' pregnant."

"You do have a talent for stating the obvious."

"You don't need money. Miranda is more than willing to take care of you, and the Lord knows she can afford it."

"I don't want or need to be taken care of! Good grief, I've been on my own since I turned eighteen." Before that, really, but that's when she legally took custody of herself.

"Yeah, but you're broke, out of work and unable to even look for a job because of your psycho boyfriend. You've got a baby to think of. I'd say you could use a little help."

He made her feel small. Small and helpless and incompetent, and she couldn't stand it. "If you call him my boyfriend again, I swear I'm going to—to—"

"Hit me?" For some stupid, male reason, that amused him. His eyes crinkled up at the corners. "Okay. Have at it."

"I don't like violence." She turned away.

At least he didn't grab her this time. And she was not the least bit disappointed that he let her go so easily, either.

Emma headed for the dining room, where an array of snacks and desserts had been laid out. At the moment, the room was empty, which was even more appealing than the chocolate raspberry cake.

Well...*almost* as appealing. She picked up one of the small dessert plates and cut a nice, big slice. Then she stood there and scowled at the piece of cake she'd slid onto her plate.

How dare Flynn Sinclair imply that she couldn't take care of herself? She'd been on her own for years and years. Maybe the mess with Steven had changed things some. Maybe she *had* to accept a little help right now. Nothing had changed permanently, she assured herself as she loaded her fork with chocolate cake dripping with raspberry sauce.

Steven would give up eventually. She'd get a job and a place of her own, maybe even here in San Antonio. She'd have her baby, and...

And then she wouldn't really be on her own anymore, would she?

Emma smiled and rubbed her tummy. Anita, or maybe Adam, was turning somersaults. No, she wouldn't be on her own anymore. She and her baby would be on *their* own—together.

It was a lovely thought.

She took a big, gooey bite. The cake was wonderful. And she was going to do just fine. Steven couldn't find her here. Good as he was, he wasn't Superman or 007. And Flynn, aggravating as he might be, was no fool. He'd make sure there was nothing in his office that gave her whereabouts away. Just in case.

"Emma," a woman said from behind her. "Emma Fortune?"

Her name was not Fortune. It was Michaels. Michaels

was a perfectly good name, even if it had come from some list kept by a social worker. But whoever was calling her no doubt meant well, so she mustered a smile as she turned, plate in hand.

A flash went off in her face. ''What the—''

''How does it feel to get rich overnight?'' that voice asked. ''What was your first thought when you found out you were a Fortune?''

She blinked, the dazzlement fading to reveal a tall, skinny woman with short black hair, a short black skirt and a tight black top. And a camera. ''Who are you?''

The woman grinned. ''The person who's about to give you your five minutes of fame, honey. Natalie Bernstein, of the *Texas Tattler*.''

Two

Ten days later

The light turned red just in time to make Flynn stomp on the brakes. He pulled to a stop, drummed his fingers impatiently on the steering wheel and glanced at the tabloid newspaper lying on the seat beside him.

Dammit to hell. The photo on the front page wasn't flattering, but it was recognizable. No one who'd ever seen that smile would fail to recognize Emma.

And just in case they had some doubts, the fool reporter had printed her name right beneath it. Oh, they'd called her "Emma Fortune" instead of Michaels, but that wasn't going to do anything more than irritate her. It sure wouldn't fool the scumbag she'd been engaged to. And the cutesy little rags-to-riches story that went with the photo identified Flynn and gave enough information for a sixth grader to find her.

Steven Shaw wasn't a sixth-grader. He was a pro.

The light changed. Flynn pulled away quickly.

Take it easy, he told himself as he turned off into the entry to the exclusive Kingston Estates, a gated community where Miranda's villa was located. Even if Shaw saw that tabloid the minute it hit the stands, he couldn't get here this fast. But the sense of urgency riding him wouldn't let up. He slowed, flashed his ID at the man at the gate, then accelerated smoothly.

It was his fault. If he'd stayed with her at the party, he could have gotten that camera away from the party-crashing reporter. If he'd followed his instincts and talked to Ryan before the party instead of waiting until he'd talked to Emma, the reporter would never have gotten in. Ryan would have seen to that.

Of course, Emma could have prevented the whole mess, too, by telling her uncle what was going on—if she weren't so blasted pigheaded.

When Flynn pulled up in front of the townhome, Emma's battered Ford was in the driveway. So was an Explorer.

Looked like Kane Fortune was here, too. Good. Flynn slammed the door to his Jeep and stalked up to the steps to the front door.

Miranda opened it herself. She was wearing a long blue robe that zipped up the front, her hair and makeup neatly fixed. She blinked when she saw him.

"I'm sorry to bother you at this hour, but I need to see Emma."

"I'm sorry. Do come in." She held the door wider and stepped back. "We're all in the breakfast room. Would you like to join us? There are muffins left, and I think some eggs, too."

"I wouldn't mind a cup of coffee." The poor lady's fingers were nervously pleating the blue silk of her robe.

Flynn did his best to look reassuring. "I imagine you can guess why I'm here."

She nodded jerkily. "The picture."

"Yeah."

"Emma thinks she has to leave. To just—take off. I hope you'll help me convince her the situation isn't that serious."

Either Miranda was living in a fantasy world, or Emma hadn't leveled with her. "Even if Shaw doesn't read the tabloids himself, odds are that someone he knows does. All it takes is for one person to mention it to him."

Her lips tightened. Without another word, she turned and led the way down a short hall.

The breakfast room was a small, sunny place. Lots of wood, painted white; lots of undraped windows with frilly things at the tops. The cushions on the chairs were green and yellow, and matched the frilly things at the windows.

Kane sat at the white table. The plate in front of him held only crumbs. He looked up when Flynn entered, his level gaze unsurprised. "You've seen that damned picture, I guess."

Flynn nodded. He was looking at the other occupant of the room, who was wearing a red cotton nightgown that buttoned up to the neck. Emma's plate held a dismembered muffin and some scrambled eggs she'd stirred around. Her hair looked like she'd stuck her head in a blender.

Her face was a little fuller, he noted with satisfaction. He couldn't tell about her arms with that enveloping nightgown, but he thought she'd put a little weight on. Good.

"Flynn! What are you doing here?" Her eyes were wide and startled.

"Having coffee," he said, going to the hutch where a pot sat on a warmer. "Then we're going to get some things straightened out."

"What's to straighten out? I've got to leave, that's all."

"Yeah, I'm afraid you do." He brought his cup over to the table and sat across from her. She looked cute with blender hair. He wondered if her breasts were that full all the time, and wished she was wearing something clingy so he could see the shape of her breasts better....

Damn. What was wrong with him?

Miranda frowned. "Even if this man does come looking for Emma, she doesn't have to leave. Kingston Estates has security."

"A bored security guard or two won't slow Shaw down, I'm afraid, if he's determined to get to Emma."

"What do you know that we don't?" Kane asked.

"That's what we need to get straight." He sipped his coffee appreciatively. "This is great coffee, Miranda. You grind it fresh?"

"I—yes."

"There's a little place on Esquivel that has some good blends. The beans are shipped vacuum-sealed. You might want to try it some time."

"You came here to talk about coffee?" Emma said sweetly.

"You want to get right to business? Okay. What have you told them about Steven Shaw?"

"Everything necessary." She met his eyes steadily, but her fingers fidgeted with the handle on her coffee cup. "I don't see what you're doing here. Why you've involved yourself in this."

"Damned if I know." He couldn't stand to think of the scumbag getting hold of her, that was all. "Except that I'm pretty sure you've held back a few important facts from your mom and your brother, here."

Those curvy eyebrows of hers sailed up haughtily. "Such as?"

"Did you tell them you needed stitches after the last time you saw Shaw? Did you mention that after beating you, he locked you in the bathroom and you had to break out before you could get medical care?''

In the silence that fell, the small, dismayed noise that Miranda made sounded very loud. Flynn noticed that the knuckles on Kane's fists were white. He sighed. ''I didn't think so.''

''You talked to Mindy. You must have. No one else—'' She shook her head. ''I trusted her.''

''Who's Mindy?'' Kane asked.

''My friend. We worked together at the florist's in San Diego and she helped me get away. I can't believe she told Flynn everything.''

''She didn't tell me. She told a colleague of mine. I told you I'd checked out your boyfriend—excuse me, your former fiancé—after I got that call from Mathers.'' He watched the expressions fleeting across her face. Dismay, maybe shame. Disbelief. Anger. ''If it makes you feel any better, Sam had a hell of a time getting her to open up.''

''Mindy knew better than to talk to a P.I.''

''Ed's good at getting people to trust him.''

Her words came out flat. ''So is Steven.''

He nodded. ''That's why you ran, isn't it? Instead of going to the cops for help. Because you didn't trust the San Diego P.D.''

''He's got buddies on the force.'' She pushed back her chair and stood.

Kane spoke up. ''Emma told us this man is a bounty hunter. I take it he's got contacts in the police department?''

''He used to be a cop,'' Flynn said, ''before he got kicked off the force for using unnecessary roughness.''

Emma froze. ''He said he'd quit the force because he hated all the red tape that keeps officers from doing their jobs.''

"Right. Red tape meaning he wasn't allowed to pistol-whip an uncooperative witness, I suppose."

"I didn't know." She ran both hands over her hair. It didn't do much to tame the unruly mass. "God. There was so much I didn't know."

She was so pale, her skin chalky with shock. He wanted to sound gentle. It came out gruff. "You wouldn't have, of course."

"The man is obviously bad news," Kane said. "But will he really chase Emma all the way to Texas?"

"Emma thinks he will. Don't you?"

"How can I be sure? He said…" She started pacing, her movements jerky. "When you were checking him out, did you find out if he's been looking for me?"

"Yeah." He hated to tell her that, but she needed to know. "Mindy told Sam he'd talked to her. And from what Sam learned, he's got feelers out elsewhere."

Her eyes closed. "I've got to get out of here."

Miranda went to her. "We'll get you protection, Emma."

"You don't understand. Steven is…once he's decided to do something, he doesn't turn back. No matter what."

That's what he'd needed to know. Flynn turned slightly in his chair to watch her restless movement, his decision made. "Mindy wasn't crazy about breaking a confidence, but when Ed explained the situation, she could see you needed help. You seem to have some trouble with that concept."

She stopped by one of the big windows, her fingers gripping the frame. "I've been accepting help for the past two months. The result was that photograph."

"That happened because you hadn't leveled with the people who want to help you. But you've made a start. The next step is to go pack your bags. I've got a fishing cabin about two hours away. We'll go there."

She stared at him. "I beg your pardon."

The corner of his mouth kicked up. "You know, you look a lot like your mom when you do that."

"I don't—oh, this is ridiculous. I'm not going anywhere with you."

Kane's eyebrows lifted. "Are you offering the use of your cabin, Flynn? Or your services as bodyguard? You don't come cheap. I'm not sure Emma can afford you."

"Money is not an issue," Miranda said crisply. "But Emma doesn't have to run off to some cabin. We can get her all the protection she needs. If she needs a body-guard—"

"I need to leave," Emma said flatly.

"Emma." Miranda spread her hands in a helpless gesture. "If this Steven Shaw is violent, the last thing you should do is take off on your own." She touched Emma's arm. "There's more than your own safety at stake now."

Even from here, Flynn could see how she tensed at her mother's touch. "I know that."

Miranda sighed. "Whatever you do, you're going to need money. Maybe this is the time to tell you that I intend to settle funds directly on you, not on my grandchild. It—it should have been yours, anyway. My father would have left you and Justin provided for if he'd known."

"No." Emma shook her head. "No, I've told you and told you—a trust fund to pay for the baby's college is fine. And I haven't had much choice except to accept a small allowance from you, since I gave up my job to come here. No one wants to hire a woman who's seven months' pregnant—especially when they see this address on my application. They don't believe I really need the work. But I can't and won't accept more than that."

Miranda smiled sadly. "Oh, Emma. What makes you think you have a choice?"

Emma's mouth opened and closed twice before she managed to say, "You can't just make me rich whether I like it or not!"

Kane broke in impatiently. "Mother doesn't need your permission. She's already spoken to her lawyer."

"But I don't have any right to her money! It should go to you, eventually. You're her son, her—" Emma closed her mouth suddenly.

Her *real* child. The last words might have gone unspoken, but every person in the room heard them anyway.

Miranda's voice was as quiet as always when she answered. But there was no missing the determination that lay behind her words. "You can do whatever you like with the money—set up a trust fund for the baby, give everything away, whatever. But it *will* be yours."

Poor waif, Flynn thought. Most people would be delirious with joy to learn they were about to be rich. Emma looked like she'd been sucker-punched.

He decided to distract the others to give her a few minutes to pull herself together. "If she does stay here, you're going to need extra security."

"What do you recommend?" Miranda asked.

"You'd need a team. Five men should do it."

Miranda's eyes widened. "So many?"

"Four to take the outside in shifts, with two on duty at all times, one in front and one out back. Plus someone who can stick with her 24-7."

"Sounds like you're arranging security for a head of state." Kane drew his eyebrows together. "Is Shaw really that dangerous?"

"He's good. Damn good, from what I hear. Sam says he's got quite a reputation on the West Coast for always bringing in his man."

Miranda gave a delicate shudder. "A bounty hunter. I suppose his job made him seem dangerous and...

interesting.'' Her tone of voice made it obvious what she thought.

Flynn glanced at Emma. She looked a hundred miles away, her brow pleated, her arms hugging her middle. He'd give her a little more time to make up her mind, he decided. She might be a flake, and stubborn as hell, but she wasn't stupid. "Not all bounty hunters are like Shaw. I've worked with some decent ones.''

"I didn't even know they existed,'' Miranda admitted. "I thought that sort of thing went out with the old West.''

"Most bounty hunters work directly for one or two bail bondsmen. Shaw's an exception. He freelances up and down the California coast. He's got a name for taking the hard cases, the skips no one can find—or wants to find, because they're too dangerous.''

"Maybe we should have him followed,'' Kane said, "instead of mounting guard on Emma. That's a temporary solution, at best.''

Miranda nodded. "Yes, that makes sense. Is that something you could handle, Mr. Sinclair?''

"You'd do better to get a California agency if you go that route. I can recommend one, if you want. But keep in mind that while putting a tail on Shaw might help, it's a temporary fix, too. If he's as good as everyone says, he'll spot the tail eventually.''

"That's not necessarily a bad thing,'' Miranda said. "If he knows that Emma has people protecting her, that he'd get caught if he did try anything, surely he would give up.''

"Maybe. Maybe not. It might just make him determined to outsmart everyone.''

"That sounds like Steven.'' That came from Emma, her voice small. She stood near the window, motionless. Slowly she turned her head to look at Flynn. "I've heard him say 'whatever it takes' any number of times.''

"You think he'll come after you.''

She nodded.

"Okay. How long will it take you to pack?"

Miranda gave him a sharp look. "But I thought we'd decided that Emma can stay here. We'll get her the security she needs."

He kept his eyes on the small, straight-backed woman by the window. "Emma hasn't decided."

"Well." She swallowed. "I wouldn't be able to pay you right away. Not until…" She grimaced. "Not until Miranda's lawyer finishes doing whatever it is lawyers do."

"I can wait."

"*I* would be your client this time. Not Miranda, or anyone else."

He nodded.

"All right, then. If you're sure you can wait to be paid, consider yourself hired."

Apparently she'd decided to trust him. Part of Flynn liked that. Part of him wanted to shake her. She had no reason to trust him. "Get packed, then. I'll be back as soon as I can, but I've got to hand off some cases. It may take a little while."

"I hadn't thought of that. If you have to give up your other cases—"

"Don't worry. The bill I give you when this is wound up will make up for any work I lose."

Miranda frowned. "Emma, stop and think. Flynn is only one man. And what do you really know about him? Aside from the fact that he was willing to work for Lloyd, that is." She obviously didn't consider that much of a recommendation. Flynn couldn't say he blamed her.

"I trust my instincts."

"I'm sure he's a good investigator, but you've got family now. Let us take care of you. If you don't want to stay with me, you could move out to the ranch, with Ryan and Lily. Or you could stay with Kane, or with Justin up in

Pittsburgh. I'm sure if he knew what was going on, he'd offer to take you in.''

It was the wrong thing to say. Emma's eyes flashed. "I don't need to be 'taken in' like a stray cat. I'll be better off somewhere Steven can't find me, which means I can't stay with—with relatives.''

Flynn noticed that she'd avoided using the word "family." "You'd better get packed," he said. "We'll leave as soon as I get back.''

She nodded. "I'll be back in a minute.''

A minute? His mouth kicked up. "If you can get packed that fast, you're not like any woman I've ever known.''

Miranda was still trying. "Emma, this is foolish.''

She gave her mother a long, level glance, but didn't answer. Instead she spoke to Flynn. "I'll be right back," she repeated, and left the room at her usual fast-forward pace.

There was a moment of silence. Miranda broke it. "I don't appreciate you luring my daughter away from her family. Are you hard up for clients, Mr. Sinclair? Or are you fixated on Emma, too?''

Flynn's jaw tightened. "I'm going to take into account that you're upset, ma'am.''

For a moment she looked her age. "I shouldn't have said that. I'm sorry. In any event, there's no need for you to wait for payment. I'll take care of your fee. If you'll wait here a moment, I'll get my checkbook.''

"Emma is my client.''

"What sort of retainer do you need? Will five thousand be enough?''

"I don't think you're listening, Ms. Fortune. Emma has hired me, not you.''

"I—'' She stopped and smoothed her robe with one nervous hand. "Yes, of course. But I'd like to pay you for—for reports.''

He raised one eyebrow. "You want me to report on my client to you? You have a funny notion of my ethics."

"I just want to know what's going on. That she's all right. Emma won't tell me. She doesn't tell me anything of importance."

"I'm sorry," he said gently. "But that's between you and her."

"But I'm her mother! Surely I have some rights!"

"No," Emma said quietly from the doorway. "You don't. You gave them up thirty-two years ago—though not officially. If you'd taken the time to relinquish custody officially, I could have been adopted by my second foster mother. *She* wanted me."

Three

"**W**e're nearly there," Flynn said as he turned off onto a roughly graded road shaded by elm and oak. "Are you going to stop pouting over losing the argument anytime soon?"

"I was sleeping, not pouting." Though she would admit to being annoyed. Flynn had refused to let her follow him here in her own car. The tags could be traced, he'd said. How? she'd asked—quite reasonably, she thought. As long as she didn't get a ticket, how could Steven find her through her car registration? But all he'd said was that if she didn't leave her rattletrap of a car behind, he wouldn't take her to his cabin.

Still, she wouldn't say she'd been pouting. Maybe she had been quieter than usual, but she had a lot on her mind, didn't she? Like Steven, and wondering how long she would have to hide from him. And her baby. That was a lovely preoccupation, but she couldn't help worrying, too.

Her life was uncertain right now. Add to that the fact that she was now dependent on a man who was practically a stranger, and who wouldn't be preoccupied?

Then there was her awkward, unrelenting awareness of the near-stranger in the seat next to her.

Flynn drove a full-size luxury car. It wasn't new, but it was comfortable, and there was more room in the front seat than in her whole car. She shouldn't have felt as if his big body ate up all the space, as if sharing the very air they breathed created some special intimacy. How silly.

How annoying.

It would be better when they reached his cabin. Once she had some privacy, she would stop being so aware of the dusting of hair on the backs of his big hands. And she wasn't going to start wondering where else hair grew on his body, either.

Impatient with herself, Emma punched the button that made her window go down. The air here was rich compared to the dry desert air she'd grown used to—damp from the lake she couldn't yet see, sweet with the intangibly green smell of spring, spiced by a whisper of flowers in bloom. "We're almost there, aren't we? What's your place like?"

"Small."

"You criticize me for sulking, but when I try to start a conversation you stop it with one word. You're a difficult man, Flynn Sinclair."

"So I've been told." The road took a sharp twist around a tightly packed cluster of young pines. "You apologized to your mother before we left."

"I don't like hurting people." And she had hurt Miranda. Again. They'd do better with a little distance between them, she thought. It would give them a chance to adjust to each other.

"Maybe not. But you were more honest before, when you made that crack about her not wanting you."

Her temples were beginning to throb. "Is there some direction you're going with this, or are you just poking at me because you're bored?"

"Hell, I don't know." He rubbed a hand over his head, and the little squiggle of a curl fell onto his forehead again.

It looked very touchable, and no more tame than the man himself. It was so black even bright sunshine failed to strike a single gleam of red or gold in its depths, black and thick, silky enough to sink right into....

"I like Miranda," he said. "She's hurting. I'd like to see the two of you work things out."

"I like her, too. The person she is now, anyway." She tipped her head to one side. "You love your mother a lot, don't you?"

He scowled. "What does that have to do with anything?"

She found his irritation perversely cheering. He didn't want to talk about his feelings or his family, did he? Just hers. "You sympathize with Miranda's feelings easily. You understand them. So I think you love your mother, and would go out of your way to protect her feelings." She smiled. "That's sweet."

"Yeah, that's me. A real sweetheart." His scowl didn't ease one jot. "Looks like we're here."

She faced forward, eager to see where she'd be living for awhile.

The house was built on a tree-studded slope that dipped down to the lake some fifty feet away. It was small, with cedar siding. Two steps led up to a front porch that held an old rocking chair and several empty flowerpots. A chimney poked out of the steeply gabled roof at one side.

It was adorable. She glanced at him and grinned. She wouldn't tell him that. He was still sulking over being called sweet. "It's lovely. I can hardly wait to see inside."

"It's nothing fancy. One big room for cooking and eating and everything else, a couple of bedrooms. That's about it.'' He pulled up in front of the house. "Electricity, but no dishwasher or microwave. No phone, but we'll have my cell phone.''

"It sounds perfect, as long as there's a bathroom you forgot to mention.'' After two hours on the road, her bladder was about to burst.

"What would you do if I said the facilities are out back?''

"Leave.'' She unfastened her seat belt. "After I buried your body, of course. You do not tell a pregnant woman she has to do without indoor plumbing.''

His mouth crooked up. "See there? You can rustle up something resembling a temper when you try.''

"And why would you want me to lose my temper?'' She climbed out and stretched. Lord, but it felt good to do that.

"Maybe I think you're cute when you're mad.''

She rolled her eyes, opened the car's back door and reached for the tote she'd stuffed everything into that hadn't fit in her suitcase. Two firm hands gripped her arms, pressed them to her sides, and moved her out of the way. Flynn stepped in front of her and reached in for her tote.

"Two months ago, I was carrying loaded trays to hungry people as fast as I could get them out. I can manage a small tote.''

"You did what you had to do,'' he said agreeably. "You don't have to do this. When I'm around, you don't lift anything heavier than your toothbrush.'' He turned, tote bag in hand, and held out a key. "Here, you can get the door open while I get the rest of the things.''

"Maybe you should carry my purse, too. It's awfully heavy.''

"You're cute when you're sarcastic, too.''

As Emma saw it, her choices were either to hit him or

ignore him and go open the door. She reminded herself that violence was never a solution, and headed for the steps.

The flower pots scattered across the rough plank floor of the porch weren't empty, after all. They held dirt and shriveled, pathetic carcasses. "Why are your plants all dead?"

"I like things simple. Dead plants are easier to take care of."

Drat the man. He'd made her grin. "I hope you don't have any pets."

"Poor Spot," he said sadly, coming up behind her. "I hope you don't have any moral objections to taxidermy."

Her head spun around. "You didn't."

"Gotcha." He grinned.

Oh, that was unfair. His face was all craggy and interesting when he wore his usual dour expression. When he grinned, the mismatched parts fell into place in an unreasonably sexy way. She jammed the key in the lock.

The inside of the little lake house wasn't as charming as the outside, but it had possibilities. The walls were paneled, the floor wooden and the furniture was bulky enough to suit a man his size. A long couch upholstered in mud-brown faced the empty fireplace, along with two shabby armchairs and a pair of beautiful end tables.

The kitchen area was at the back of the long everything-room. It had the usual appliances, all of them old, and a truly splendid oak table big enough to feed a gaggle of friends and relatives.

But Flynn hadn't been feeding any crowds here. There were only two mismatched chairs at the table. They looked lonely.

The back wall, off the kitchen, was mostly glass. It opened onto another porch, this one screened. Emma smiled and drifted that way. "I like your house, Flynn. And I love the view." She turned to share her smile with him, and caught him looking at her legs. At least, if she hadn't been seven months' pregnant, she would have sworn he was checking her out.

But that was ridiculous, under the circumstances. "It's peaceful here. Did you pick this side of the lake so you'd see dawn breaking over the water in the mornings?"

"My father built the house. I can't ask him why he picked this spot because he's dead."

"Now, there's a real conversation stopper."

"Sorry." He ran his hand over his hair again. "To tell the truth, it feels funny having you here. I'm used to having the place to myself."

"Then I'm doubly grateful that you asked me."

"Good. Grateful clients pay promptly." He turned. "Your room's this way."

Emma followed him to a room just big enough for the double bed and dresser it held. The walls were painted instead of paneled, and the bedspread and curtains were a practical green-and-tan plaid.

"It's not fancy," he said again, putting the suitcase and tote on the floor by the bed. "But the mattress is good."

"That's all I ask. Well, that and indoor plumbing." Which she would need to visit in the near future. "What are the house rules?"

"House rules? This isn't a college dorm."

"No, but it helps to know what drives the other person batty if we're going to live together. I'm a morning person, for instance, but I like things quiet when I first get up. I'm not too crazy about CNN, but I can always take a walk if you're a news addict. What pulls your chain? Do you hate rock music, dishes left in the sink or undies hung over the shower curtain to dry?"

He shifted his feet uncomfortably. "There's no television, so that won't be an issue. I can't think of any rules except for the obvious one—you don't go anywhere without me. Not unless I okay it."

She grimaced. "That's a P.I. rule, not a house rule. Not used to sharing space, are you?"

"It's been a lot of years since I had to."

More and more, she got the impression Flynn was a loner. He had only two chairs at that huge table. He wasn't used to living with others underfoot. And he had a family, but he didn't want to talk about them.

Steven had been a loner, too. She fought back a shiver. "Well, if I do something that bugs you, just let me know." She reached for her suitcase, ready to start unpacking. "I'm adaptable."

"*That* bugs me. I told you not to lift things." He pushed her hand away and grabbed the suitcase. "I guess you've had to learn to adapt, living in so many places."

"I guess I have, but being flexible doesn't mean I'm a wimp. Stop ordering me around."

"Did you take orders from Steven? Is that why you're so prickly?"

"I wasn't a doormat," she snapped. "I may have gotten in over my head, but I got myself out, too."

"If you say so." He swung the suitcase up on the bed. "The bathroom's right through there." He nodded at a door on the wall opposite the bed. "My bedroom is on the other side, and it has a door to the bathroom, too. Which makes me think of one house rule. Don't go in the bathroom without knocking. Neither door locks."

She had a sudden image of walking in on Flynn in the shower. He would be a shower person, she felt sure, too impatient for baths. She could easily imagine the way water would run down that broad chest, trickling through the hair she was almost sure would be there....

"I'll be sure to knock," she said briskly, ignoring her warm cheeks.

Flynn didn't often sing out loud because his voice could crack glass at twenty paces, but he liked to hum or whistle.

He was humming along with the radio as he headed down FM 1210 towards the cabin for the second time that day. The sun was setting, and making a grand, splashy job of it, too, scattering reds and golds all over the western sky. He wondered if Emma was outside, watching the sunset. She seemed to have a yen for pretty things.

He wasn't worried about leaving her alone. The whole point of bringing her to his cabin was to tuck her where Shaw couldn't find her, and he'd been very, very careful to leave no trail for the son of a bitch to follow.

It felt strange to be headed for the cabin, though, knowing someone was waiting there for him. The memories attached to the place had been too painful for his step-mother. And his sisters were city girls…and, he had to admit, he'd pretty much ordered them not to visit him at the cabin. It had been his place, his alone, after their father's death. He'd needed that, needed a place where he wasn't responsible for anyone but himself.

Emma was one hell of a responsibility, though, wasn't she?

But she was a professional responsibility, he reminded himself, not a personal one, so that was all right. She wasn't like his sisters, either. She wouldn't start leaning, clinging, expecting him to fix everything for her.

No, the woman was so blasted stuck on independence she could teach college courses on the subject.

She was damned well going to let him do any heavy work. That wasn't negotiable. But any man worth his jockstrap would do that sort of thing for a woman in Emma's condition. That was as far as his involvement went, he assured himself as he turned off onto the dirt road. Flynn had waited a long time—years—to get his life where it belonged to no one but him. No way was he going to snarl things up by taking some lost waif under his wing.

Except professionally, of course. That was different.

The back seat held three sacks of groceries. Flynn had left Emma with the suggestion—he'd been careful to make it a suggestion, not an order—that she rest up while he picked up something for supper in Marble Falls.

Making a run to the market in Marble Falls on his first day at the cabin was a tradition. Years ago, it had been his father and him who'd driven in to pick up steaks while his mother and sisters unpacked. Then he and his dad would grill the steaks, giving the girls a night off.

He made the run to the market alone now, but that was how he wanted it. Only this time, in addition to the traditional steaks, potatoes and beer, he'd bought vegetables. That's what Emma had asked for, all she'd wanted from the store—plenty of fresh vegetables.

All she'd wanted at the cabin was a good bed and indoor plumbing. Her lack of demands irritated him. She deserved more from life. She should insist on more.

But then, life had never given her much. Not a mother or a family, and precious little in the way of material goods. Just a baby on the way—and a crazy bounty hunter for the baby's father.

His fingers tightened on the steering wheel. No way was that son of a bitch getting near Emma. He'd see to it. And it was none of his business what she'd seen in the man, he reminded himself as he negotiated one of the deeper ruts in the dirt road. For some reason he was curious—intensely curious—about that, though.

But curiosity was his besetting sin, wasn't it? Nothing unusual about that. He'd gotten into the P.I. business in the first place because he liked digging beneath the surface of things, making sense of a puzzle when half the pieces were missing. Still, he didn't have to know why his client had fallen for Shaw in order to do his job.

She'd been willing to marry the man. She must have had

strong feelings for him. He was brooding about that when he rounded the stand of elms and saw the cabin. And Emma.

She was scrubbing the front porch.

His temper hit boiling point before the car came to a full stop. He threw open the door and didn't bother to slam it shut behind him. "What in the hell do you think you're doing?"

She sat back on her heels, cradling her belly with one hand. The other hand held a scrub brush. She'd pulled her hair back in a braid, but it was rebelling against that confinement, fizzing around here and there in ornery curls. Her eyes were calm, her smile amused. "That's pretty obvious, isn't it?"

"I didn't bring you here so I could have maid service."

"It's a habit. I feel more at home in a place after I've given it a good cleaning."

That punctured his balloon. His anger drained out, leaving him feeling foolish. He made one more try at reasoning with her. "You're supposed to be resting after the drive."

She'd worked up a sweat with her cleaning. One of those rebellious curls clung to her cheek in a damp, wiggly question mark. "Flynn, it was a two-hour drive, not twelve. And I dozed for most of the way. I didn't need to rest, I needed to *do* something. I didn't think I should take a walk—I didn't want you to worry if you came back and I was gone. So I started cleaning."

Maybe he'd overreacted. "What's the point in scrubbing a porch, though?" Porches were always dirty. It was their nature.

"I thought I might like to meditate here in the mornings, and I didn't want to sit in bird droppings. Or I might try on the back porch. The energy is very smooth there, and the view is wonderful."

"You meditate." He sighed. "I should have known. And all those vegetables—?"

She grinned. "You guessed it. I prefer a mostly vegetarian diet, though I eat some fish and chicken. Don't look so alarmed. I won't make you eat your veggies if you don't want to. And, like I told you earlier, I'm a great cook."

She wouldn't want him to grill a steak for her, then. He was unreasonably disappointed. "Tofu stuff?"

"I can fix that, sure. But I also fix a great spaghetti sauce, and my roast chicken with dressing makes grown men weep with delight."

He was sure that wasn't the only thing she could do that might make a man weep. Or shout. He shifted uneasily, remembering why he'd been in such a hurry to leave earlier.

It was understandable that a pregnant woman would arouse his protective instincts. Lust, however, was not acceptable. No matter how cute she looked with her round tummy and curvy breasts and that squiggle of hair plastered to her cheek. "I'll get the groceries. You can show me how good you are tomorrow. At cooking, I mean." Definitely at cooking. He took a slow breath. "I've got steaks to grill tonight. If you don't eat red meat, you're going to find the meal a little skimpy."

"We can toss some vegetables on the grill, too. They're great that way." She slapped idly at her arm.

"You know, it's getting on towards dusk. I really think you should go inside soon."

"You do, huh?" When she tilted her head, that curl finally came loose and dangled in her eyes. She brushed it back.

He nodded slowly. "I'm not telling you what to do, mind you. Just offering an opinion. It all depends on how you like your mosquitoes—in small, intimate groups, or a big party crowd."

"I'm not much of a party girl. Especially if the guests consider my blood the refreshments. I guess the porch is clean enough." She twisted and dropped the scrub bush in the nearby bucket. "You going to let me help you bring the groceries in?"

"That depends. You going to let me help you to your feet?" He held out a hand.

Her smile slipped, then came back, brighter than ever. "Sure. Contrary to your opinion, I'm perfectly capable of accepting a helping hand. It takes a pretty good heave to get me up from the floor these days."

The second he closed his fingers around hers, something happened. Something like an electrical storm, complete with a wind that blew right through him, sudden and swift and silent. A hot wind. Skin-stinging hot.

He almost dropped her hand. Some gritty remnant of a thought reminded him of what he was supposed to be doing, so he gave her a pull. She didn't weigh all that much, even now, and came to her feet easily—and then stood there, her hand still in his, her eyes huge and her smile blown away by that hot wind.

Or maybe he was imagining that she'd felt it, too. He hoped to God he was. "I got plenty of vegetables," he said, dropping her hand and making a beeline for the car. He slammed the front door he'd left open, opened the back door, and dived after one of the sacks. "Hope you like broccoli."

"Oh, yes, broccoli. That's great. I love broccoli. How about you?"

"The only green food I like is mint ice cream. I got some of that."

"Mint ice cream is good." She nodded vigorously, making that wayward curl dance. "I love mint ice cream. Not that I would eat it if you want it yourself."

"No, you're welcome to have some." *Get a grip, Sin-*

clair. "I left one of the bags for you." The one with the bread and eggs and toilet paper. It weighed less than that purse she lugged around.

"Great. Well, let's get these inside."

"Sure thing."

It hadn't been his imagination. Her too-bright smile and nervous chatter announced plainly that she'd been zapped as well, and wasn't any crazier about it than he was. Good. They were both adults, right? They'd ignore this stupid attraction, and after awhile it would go away.

He was so busy congratulating himself on this piece of logic that he didn't notice she'd stopped in the doorway, her head turned toward him as if she were about to say something. He stopped barely in time to keep from mowing her down.

Their arms brushed. Their bodies would have, too, if they hadn't had all those wonderful grocery sacks between them. Her eyes got a blind, panicky look in them. Heat swirled through his body.

"Sorry," he muttered.

"Sorry," she echoed, and took off for the kitchen like a cat with a pack of dogs on her tail.

In a pinch, there was always the lake, he reminded himself. Lots and lots of nice, cold water where he could go soak his head...and other parts.

Four

Early the next morning, Emma sat cross-legged on the back porch and hummed her *om*. It didn't help. Her mind wouldn't be still. It jumped all over the place, quick and busy as a water bug dodging hungry bass.

The rest of the world was peaceful. The sky was waking up slowly, light stretching across the water in soft peach fingers that faded into whispery blue overhead, turning indigo in the west. Birds twittered and chirped. Small waves, gentle as an afterthought, lapped at the shore. Even Nancy—or maybe Adrian—was quiet, for once not practicing drop-kicks.

But she'd made the mistake of leaving the sliding doors open when she came out here, and she smelled coffee. And knew that, on the other side of the glass, Flynn Sinclair was sitting at his big, lonely table in a pair of jeans...and nothing else. She'd noticed that when she walked across the kitchen, heading for the porch.

He did have hair on his chest, just as she'd thought. Not too much, just a nice, inky-dark thatch right in the center of a well-muscled chest, hair that did the arrow thing, tapering to a point that disappeared into the waistband of his jeans.

Drat the man. Why couldn't he have been a night owl who slept till noon every day? Or ugly. Ugly would definitely have helped. Maybe then she wouldn't have humiliated herself yesterday.

He'd seen. Oh, yes, he'd seen her reaction to him. He'd kept his distance the rest of the evening, exquisitely careful not to allow a chance touch to ignite her pathetically combustible hormones again. Finally she'd taken pity on them both and gone to bed.

Emma took a deep, calming breath. *Ommmm...*

There was a dock where Flynn's property joined the lake, and a big, tin-roofed boat shed. She wondered what kind of boat he had. One of those snazzy fiberglass speedboats, all glitter and gleam? Maybe a bass boat, the kind with a shallow draft and deep, cushy seats. Or...

Oh, never mind. She might as well put her thoughts to work, since they refused to shut off. With a sigh, Emma unfolded her legs and got them into position for the chore of standing up. Her center of balance was seriously skewed these days.

By the time she reached her feet, Flynn was standing in the doorway, holding out a steaming cup.

"Oh," she said wistfully. "I can't drink coffee. Caffeine is bad for the baby."

"It's one of those funny teas women like. No caffeine."

She came closer, took the mug and inhaled deeply, enjoying the spicy smell more, she knew, than she would the taste. Emma liked the idea of tea better than she did the drinking of it. In spite of her efforts to acquire a taste for tea, deep down she craved coffee.

But she couldn't have coffee now, and it had been terribly sweet of him to make her a cup of tea. She beamed at him. "I'm surprised you had some tea sitting around. Thank you."

"I picked it up yesterday at the store. Seemed like it would go with all those vegetables you wanted." His grin was slow and teasing. "Seems like you do everything in a hurry. Your meditating didn't take very long."

"Usually I meditate for half an hour, but I couldn't get out of my monkey mind this morning. I decided I might as well put it to work." She took a sip of the steaming tea. It wasn't bad, really. A blend of citrus and spice.

"Your, uh, monkey mind." He made it a statement, not a question, as if he wasn't sure he wanted her to explain.

"The rational, thinking part of the mind."

"As opposed to the stupid part?"

She chuckled. "As opposed to the nonthinking part, what you might call the subconscious. The nonverbal brain, where dreams, hunches and intuition are born."

"Nothing wrong with a hunch or two, but I prefer rationality when I'm awake."

"I'm sure you do." Amused, she took another sip. "This is pretty good. Anyway, I was thinking when I was supposed to be meditating, and one of the things I was thinking about was how temporary this is. Me staying here, I mean. I can't hide forever."

He'd brought his coffee out with him. She managed not to sigh with coffee-envy when he lifted the mug to his lips. "True," he said. "I've got some ideas about that, but I haven't put anything together yet. Hasn't been time."

"What kind of ideas?"

"I don't talk about a plan until I have the pieces checked out and in place."

"I *am* your client."

He nodded amiably. "So you are. And just as soon as I

have something to report, I will. Until then, it's none of your business.''

How could she have been lusting after this muleheaded throwback to a caveman? "Fine. I have an idea, too. It's a little rough, and of course I couldn't do anything until after the baby is born, but maybe you can help me work out the details.''

Excited about her plan, she started to move. The back porch ran the width of the house and was as cluttered as the inside was tidy. She stepped around a clutch of fishing poles near the screen door. "If Steven stalks me or attacks me, that's against the law, right?''

"Of course." He carried his coffee over to the picnic table where they'd eaten last night, hitching a hip against it. "But until he does something, the law can't act.''

"Exactly.'' She dodged a big table saw. "So we have to see to it he gets caught breaking the law.''

His eyebrows went up. "I've been thinking along the same lines.''

"You have?'' Pleased, she paused by a stack of lumber. "Then you agree? The only way to stop Steven is to catch him in the act. We'd have to let him figure out where I am. Then, when he comes after me, we'll have a trap set, and bam!'' She smacked her hands together. "Got him.''

"God help me.'' He straightened and thunked his mug down on the table. "You'd better go back to meditating. Rationality is not your strong suit. Where did you get a lamebrained idea like that? Some stupid cop show on TV?''

"I never watch TV. Well, except for *Buffy,* and sometimes the Discovery Channel, but—''

"Stick with the Discovery Channel.'' He shook his head, disgusted. "You are going to be a mother. You can't take risks like that.''

"I was talking about after the baby is born,'' she explained patiently. "I thought I said that. Obviously I can't take any chances now, and it will be hard to be away from my baby when we're setting the trap. But I can do whatever I have to.''

''Forget it. You aren't risking yourself, and that's all there is to it.''

''The risk shouldn't be that great, not if we set things up right.''

''So you think it's okay to take a chance of leaving your kid without a mother?''

Abigail or Jerry chose that moment to stretch. A small head pressed against Emma's diaphragm while two little feet tried to dig out through her pelvis.

She rubbed her middle, a fierce wave of love rising to steady her. She would do anything, anything at all, to keep her baby safe. ''I'm risking worse than that right now. Every day Steven is free, I'm taking a huge risk, whether I want to or not. He doesn't want me dead. He wants to *keep* me...but not my baby. H-he—the last time I saw him, he—'' Memories crowded in, dark and choking, built of panic and pain and blood.

''Don't.'' His voice was softer now, and he moved close. ''You don't need to talk about it.''

But memory had her now, twisting her along its dark paths. ''You wanted to know what I saw in him. He was good to me. Sweet, romantic...and possessive. Should I have known that was wrong, for him to be so possessive?'' She shook her head, baffled. ''He wanted to keep me. Forever. No one had ever...oh, I knew he had problems, but who doesn't? He needed me. I didn't know how bad his problems were. I really didn't know.''

He put his hands on her arms and rubbed them. It was such a brisk sort of comforting that she almost smiled. ''Of course you didn't.''

''I should have. But he didn't turn violent until I told him I was pregnant. And then—then he just smiled at me,

the same as always. And told me to get rid of it.'' The
shock of that moment was still with her. Steven had such
a sweet smile…. ''When I refused—when I realized—''
She closed her eyes and finished in a whisper. ''He tried
to beat my baby out of me. He hated the baby. Not me.
My *baby*.''

Flynn pulled her up against him. He was so much taller
than she was, so much harder. Her tummy nestled comfortably against him. One of his big hands soothed her
shoulders, and her breath shivered out in a sigh.

She felt safe. And warm. And tingly, damn it. Too warm
for comfort, too safe to move.

''Sugar, he's not going to get near you. That's what I'm
here for. That bastard won't get within spitting distance of
you. You don't have to choose between your safety and
your baby's.''

''You won't be around forever.'' No one stayed forever.
They all left, sooner or later…. ''I need a permanent solution.''

''Like I said, I've got some ideas. With Shaw's reputation for—''

''Flynn, you lazy son of a bitch!'' a deep voice boomed
from inside the house. ''Saw your car in the drive, so I
know you're here. Get your butt out of bed, boy. The sun
is up and the fish are biting.''

Emma pulled away, looking around wildly. Through the
windows she saw a huge man stood at the far end of the
great room, near the door. He wore a ball cap, jeans that
rode well below his overhanging belly and a dark T-shirt.

Flynn dropped his arms and raised his voice. ''I'm on
the back porch, Martin.''

''Who is that?'' she whispered.

''My neighbor. He's got a key.'' Flynn sighed. ''Unfortunately.''

The big man had to open the glass doors wider to join

them, and the porch shook slightly when he did. He was tall—taller even than Flynn—and broad. Well, fat, really, though she had the impression there was a lot of muscle beneath that fat. Gray hair stuck out in wild tufts from beneath a blue ball cap that read Big S Welding. The grizzled stubble on his face was gray, too. His grin was wide enough to swallow half the state.

"Emma, this is Martin Sandowski. He's the best fisherman in the county, even if he does have muscle between his ears instead of brains."

The insult made Martin's grin wider. "Got enough muscles elsewhere to whup your puny butt. Show some respect for your elders." He gave Emma a friendly nod. "Pleased to meet you, ma'am. Can't imagine what you're doing here with this reprobate."

He had Santa Claus eyes, she decided—blue, merry and shrewd. He was curious, but he wasn't staring or judging. She liked that. "At the moment, I'm going to fix him some eggs. Would you like to join us for breakfast, Mr. Sandowski?"

"I only bought a dozen eggs," Flynn muttered.

"Pay no mind to the boy. And call me Martin. When a pretty young thing like you starts 'mister-ing' me, I worry that I might be getting old." His chuckle rumbled up from deep inside. "And I'd love to have a bite, if it's not too much trouble."

"No trouble at all," she assured him.

"If you're staying for more than a day or two, I'll have a chance to repay the hospitality. Nothing like skillet-fried catfish fresh from the lake."

"He serves his fish seasoned with tall tales," Flynn said. "You're supposed to listen wide-eyed and pretend to believe him."

Martin gave Flynn's arm a friendly punch that would have felled a smaller man. "Stories make everything go down better. Speaking of which, I'm thinking you have a story to tell, yourself.''

Emma's eyes met Flynn's. What would he say about her presence here? People would see her looking like she was ready to deliver any day now—and living with Flynn. She hadn't thought about how awkward that would be for him. ''Mr. Sandowski—Martin, I mean. You should know that the baby isn't Flynn's. I'm in a difficult situation, and he's helping me, that's all.''

''Great.'' Flynn looked disgusted. ''Just great. How long do you think we're going to keep you hidden if you tell everyone you meet your life story?''

''That's hardly my life story!'' Emma protested.

Martin's round face looked surprisingly stern. ''If you don't think I can be trusted, maybe I should pass on breakfast.''

''Dammit, I trust you. I was going to fill you in myself, but Emma didn't know that when she opened her mouth.''

''Well, then, there's no problem, and no call for you to go huffing and puffing at Emma, whose only fault is being nice enough to worry about my opinion of you.''

She beamed at him. ''How do you like your eggs, Martin?''

He gave one of those belly-deep chuckles. ''Cooked.''

Flynn looked from one to the other of them and shook his head. ''You'd better fry up some of that bacon, too. Hell, fix the whole package. Martin will start gnawing on the plate if you don't put enough food on it.''

''Watch your language,'' Martin told him. ''There's a lady present.''

''So what's going on?'' Martin asked, settling his bulk at the picnic table while Emma bustled around the kitchen, out of hearing range.

''She's a client.'' Flynn brought his coffee over to the

table and sat across from his old friend. He shouldn't have been surprised that Emma and Martin hit it off so well. Hadn't he watched her charming every customer in the truck stop where he'd found her? "And she's hip-deep in trouble."

"Unmarried and pregnant spells trouble sometimes."

Martin, of course, had noticed the lack of a ring. The man might look like a good old boy who couldn't see beyond his beer belly, but there wasn't much he missed. Retirement didn't erase forty-five years in law enforcement. "She was engaged to a bastard named Steven Shaw, a bounty hunter out in California. He's the type that gives the rest a bad name. He put Emma in the hospital before she got away. She thinks he'll come after her, and she may be right—especially once he learns that she's a Fortune by birth."

Martin's eyebrows lifted. "Is she, now? You'd better fill me in."

He did. Briefly, because he wanted to be done before Emma called them in to eat, but he knew how to hit all the important points even in a quick report. Martin had taught him that, among other things.

And while he talked, he watched Emma bustling around the kitchen. She was wearing shorts and an enormous, tie-dyed T-shirt this morning, so he could see that she had put some weight on. Not much, but her arms weren't so skinny anymore. Her legs, now…he didn't see a difference there, but her legs had been damn near perfect already.

"She is a pretty little thing, isn't she?" Martin said.

"She's a client." A man would have to be three-days dead not to notice legs like that. It didn't mean he was going to hit on her.

"Right. I guess you want me to keep my ear to the ground, maybe have a chat with Pete so he'll watch for someone matching Shaw's description."

Flynn nodded. Pete Dobson was a former deputy of Martin's, now the sheriff. Pete didn't like Flynn, didn't like any private cops, an attitude shared by a lot of law enforcement types. But he'd walk backwards if Martin suggested that was the best way to do his job. "Between Pete and your fishing buddies, I don't see how Shaw could show up within ten miles of here without someone spotting him."

"I'll put the word out. What are you planning on doing about Shaw?"

"Maybe I'll be lucky and not have to do anything. Sooner or later, the law is bound to catch up with a bounty hunter who operates the way Shaw does. He won't be a threat if he's doing five to ten for assault."

"I'd like to say I've got faith in the system, and, on the whole, I do. But later isn't always as good as sooner."

"I know. Emma has some powerful relatives. I'm in touch with them." Ryan Fortune was a man who knew how to take care of his own. He had the money, and Flynn had the contacts and some ideas about what to do. "And that's probably as much as a law-and-order type like you needs to know for now."

"Hmm. Well, chances are Shaw won't show up here. You wouldn't have left a trail."

It was a statement, not a question, which made Flynn feel foolishly pleased. "Emma's family knows she's with me, but they don't know where we are, not specifically. They can get in touch through my cell phone or my secretary. Maude knows where I am, of course, but she wouldn't tell the president where to find the bathroom if I didn't okay it ahead of time."

"Might not tell him even then, just point the way. That woman's tighter with words than a miser is with gold." He shook his head, marveling. "Can't resist a quiet, restful woman. One of these days, I'm gonna bring her around to marrying me."

No one but Martin would describe Flynn's battleax of a secretary as restful. Flynn didn't know what the relationship was between the two, and wouldn't ask. He did know Martin had proposed and been turned down more than once. "Good thing for me she's got better sense."

"She's a stubborn woman." Martin sighed, exhaling a bushel or two of air. "Thinks she wouldn't like it in the country. Now I ask you—how can she know that, when she's never tried it?"

Flynn shook his head. "It's a puzzle, all right. Of course, knowing Maude, I expect she's asked you why you're so sure you'd hate living in San Antonio. Seeing as how you've never tried it."

"I'm not giving up." Shrewd blue eyes twinkled. "Maybe I'll end up moving to San Antone."

Flynn snorted. "Yeah, I'll believe that you're moving to the big city about the same time I hear you've had a sex-change operation."

"If you knew half as much as you think you do, you'd be a real threat. When a man finds the right woman, he's got to be willing to make some compromises."

It occurred to Flynn that Martin sounded serious. That shook him. "You don't mean that. How many years did you talk about retiring onto your property here, spending your days fishing, before you did just that? You've got everything the way you always wanted it. Why would you even think about changing that?"

"Not quite the way I wanted it. I always figured on retiring with Mary. After she died, I stayed stuck on doing things they way we'd planned. A man gets used to thinking a certain way, and doesn't want to change. Now, don't go shuffling your feet and looking constipated." Martin slapped Flynn on the back. "Part of me's gonna miss Mary till the day I die, but I'm not pining anymore." He chuckled. "Except after Maude. Point is, sometimes what we want changes. Take you, for example."

"Bad example." Flynn swallowed the last of his coffee and set the mug down. "I know what I want. And I'm happy to say I've got it."

Life was just about perfect these days. He had enough work to keep him busy, enough money to take off and fish when he wanted to, an old friend to trade tall tales with. There were women from time to time, of course. Flynn couldn't imagine life without one or two of the soft, sweet-smelling creatures around. But while his relationships were always friendly, they were always temporary. Casual and easy, that's the way he liked things. And, dammit, with his sisters finally grown up, he'd earned the right to live that way.

"Yeah, that's what I figured you thought." Martin chuckled and heaved to his feet. "You probably believe that pretty filly heading this way to tell us breakfast is ready is just a client, too."

Flynn was amused. "Just because you're dreaming of orange blossoms, don't feel obliged to toss some my way. They won't stick." Lusting after a client was pointless. Lusting after a woman who bristled with strings the way this one did was downright stupid, and Flynn wasn't a stupid man. Now that he was aware of the problem, he would take steps to limit it.

As long as he kept his hands off her, he would be fine.

Five

"Leave the dishes, sugar," Flynn said. "Sit down and have some of your tea."

"They'll just take a moment," Emma assured him, squirting soap in the sink and turning the tap on high.

He'd noticed how lousy she was at following instructions. She wasn't much better at sitting still. The woman was either asleep or she was busy. He set his notebook on the table. "I need to ask you some questions about Shaw."

She froze for a second. Then her eyes cut to Martin.

"Martin was sheriff here for more years than you've been alive. He knows everyone. He's going to pass the word for folks to keep an eye out for you old boyfriend."

"Former fiancé."

"Right. He needs to know more about Shaw if he's going to help. So do I."

"I didn't mean...I guess you told him about Steven, and that's okay. That's fine. But I don't see what I can tell you that will help. You said you checked him out already."

"I did. But I don't have the kind of details you can give me." Flynn didn't like pressing her. It was obvious that thinking about the man upset her. But Emma had lived with Shaw, been ready to marry him. Flynn needed the small, intimate details that only she could provide.

She turned to the sink, dunking the dishes in one by one. Beneath the swirls of sunset colors in her tie-dyed T-shirt, her back was stiff and straight. And beneath the hems of the pink shorts, her legs were magnificent. Flynn stifled a sigh and dragged his mind back on track.

"What kind of details?" she asked when she had all the dishes buried in the soapy water.

"What he likes to eat. Mannerisms, like playing with a cigarette lighter or biting his fingernails. Friends, relatives...the man who checked him out for me didn't find anything on his family."

"He doesn't have one. Steven was a foster kid. That's one of things we had in common. He had it a lot rougher than me, though."

Flynn didn't want to hear about how the poor guy had been abused. Maybe he had been. It didn't excuse what he'd done to Emma. "Habits? Mannerisms?"

"He's very controlled. I can't think of anything...oh, he does like to chew gum. He quit smoking a few years ago."

Flynn make a note of that. "What does he do to relax? Play pool, read dirty magazines, watch sports on TV?"

"He'd rather be doing than watching, and he isn't much into team sports. Kick-boxing, karate, rock climbing—that sort of thing is more his speed. He likes to compete. He enjoys cooking, too," she added, swishing a plate under the tap to rinse it. "He's a vegetarian."

"You've got to be kidding. A vegetarian bounty hunter?"

She glanced over her shoulder. A spark of genuine

amusement lit her eyes. "He lives in California, remember?"

"Yeah, he looks like a California boy."

"You've seen a picture of him?"

"A copy of his driver's license photo." Wasn't there some kind of natural law that driver's license pictures had to be ugly as spit? Not Stephen Shaw's. "I need to get a more recent photo from you, though. Something I can copy."

"I don't have any pictures of him." She was scrubbing the frying pan as if she had to get it ready to star in a dish soap commercial. "He hated to be photographed."

"I suppose you're going to tell me he's modest, as well as having a black belt in karate." And climbing mountains for relaxation. Oh, yeah, Shaw was a real macho man—one who ate vegetables, just like Emma did.

And beat up on women.

"Modest?" She set the pan in the drainer and turned around. "No. Not that. Steven lives in a black-and-white world, and he thinks he's perfect. He has to believe that, or the monsters inside will eat him."

Her words created a hard silence, the kind that hits when the weather shifts or a gun goes off. She was hurting, Flynn realized. She was still hurting over that bastard. "Too late," he said flatly. "He *is* the monster."

"I know." Her eyes were huge and sad. "It's what he feared most."

His lip curled. "You feeling sorry for him?"

"Shut up, Flynn." There wasn't a trace of good ol' boy in Martin's voice. His chair scraped against the wooden floor as he pushed it back. "Guess I'll be going. Thanks for breakfast, Emma."

"It was my pleasure." She dried her hands on a towel and held one out.

Instead of shaking it, Martin took it and tucked it into

the crook of his arm. "Walk me to the door so I have something nicer to look at than Flynn's ugly face. I'll holler in a day or two when I've got a nice mess of catfish."

"I love fish." She smiled up at him. "Baked, fried, grilled, pretty much any way you can fix it except raw. I never could warm up to sushi."

"Only one way to fix fresh catfish. Drag it through cornmeal and pop it in a hot iron skillet."

"Fried is the only way Martin knows how to fix anything," Flynn muttered.

They ignored him, billing and cooing over catfish as they headed for the front door. "You'll let me know what I should bring," Emma said.

"Just your sweet self. Tell the boy to bake us some brownies for dessert."

Flynn scowled and moved to the sink to rinse out his mug. He heard the front door open and close, and shut off the water. Damn, but he hated being in the wrong.

"Martin wants you to bake brownies." Emma sounded amused.

He turned. "I heard. You and he sure hit it off."

"Not everyone thinks I'm an idiot. Oh—" She waved a hand dismissively. "Never mind. Talking about Steven makes me weird. Let's talk about something else." She glanced around. "Like what I'm supposed to do here all day."

"In a minute. I'm sorry."

She shrugged and moved over to the counter. "It doesn't matter. You do have a radio, I see. Mind if I find some music?"

"Martin was right to tell me to shut up. I shouldn't have made that crack about your feelings for Shaw." He closed the distance between them.

Her shoulders looked tight beneath the soft knit of her T-shirt. "I'm not much for apologies, but if it makes you feel better to hear you've been forgiven, then fine. I'm not mad.'' She poked the power button, and the Dixie Chicks began singing about a cold day in July. ''You like country music?''

''I wouldn't have it on that station if I didn't. Why don't you like apologies? Women are usually nuts about getting a guy to say he's sorry.'' His sisters sure reveled in it if they managed to wring an apology from him.

''They seem pretty useless, that's all. I don't believe in holding on to negative feelings, especially with friends.''

''You forgive everyone for everything?'' Thinking of what Shaw had done made his voice came out harder than he wanted. ''No matter what?''

''No.'' She turned around slowly. ''I'm no saint. I try to let the small stuff roll off me, but if someone does something really wrong, really hurtful, an apology won't help, will it?''

''Sometimes it can.'' Her skin was about as perfect as anything he'd ever seen, he thought. Soft and warm and smooth as the lake at dawn. ''Sometimes it opens things up enough for people to talk.''

''Talking doesn't always help.''

Her eyes looked so soft and sad. And stubborn. Her lips were soft, too, maybe even softer than that pale, pretty skin. And her mouth was small. Funny, but he hadn't realized that before. Maybe it was because she smiled so much, and when she smiled, her whole face got into the act. That all-over smile kept a man from noticing how small and alarmingly soft her mouth really was. ''You're not a wimp. You're too stubborn for that. But you're too blasted soft, Emma. You give too much, too easily.''

''You ought to know.'' There was that smile now, spreading over her face, making her eyes the merriest blue he'd ever seen. ''You're a giver, too.''

His eyebrows snapped down. ''I am not.''

"Sure you are." She patted his cheek. "Why else did you bring me here?"

There was a reason. There was undoubtedly a sound, sensible reason, because he was a sensible man. Right this moment, he couldn't think of what it was. "You shouldn't do that."

"What?"

"Touch me. Trust me. Dammit, you don't have any reason to trust me."

Color washed over her cheeks. "I didn't mean…I'm a touchy-feely person, that's all. And of course I trust you."

"You shouldn't. You shouldn't look at me like that, either. With your eyes so big and trusting, as if you wouldn't mind if I…" Somewhere along the line, he forget what he was saying. Forgot to pay attention to what his hands did, too, because one of them lifted to touch that warm cheek.

Soft. Even softer than he'd imagined, like a mare's nose or a baby's bottom. Soft as only the innocent and defenseless can be.

She shivered.

Flynn's reaction was instant, and anything but innocent. Without thinking, without hurrying, he lowered his head. He was a breath away from tasting that pretty mouth when the phone rang.

He froze. His eyes widened in shock at what he'd been about to do. Without speaking, he stepped back, turned away, and went to get his phone. And all the while his heart was pounding and his blood was singing. And that terrible, hot wind was blowing through him again.

Flynn was avoiding her. He'd been avoiding her ever since he didn't kiss her in the kitchen two weeks ago.

It was amazing, really. Emma tucked her left foot onto her right knee and wrestled a sock on. It took a fair dose of ingenuity for the man to keep his distance, under the circumstances. But he managed. He'd used Martin as a buffer when possible. Emma did enjoy the older man's company, but she felt sure that wasn't why Flynn had encouraged him to visit so often. When Martin was there, Flynn could take off—fishing, hiking, whatever he could find to do outside the cabin, away from her.

Inside the cabin he found things to keep him busy, too. He'd brought a laptop computer with him, and spent a lot of time doing mysterious Internet things involving a couple of cases. Apparently some detecting was done online nowadays.

When he wasn't working with the computer, he was working with wood. Flynn did incredible things with wood. He'd made that gorgeous dining table himself, and the end tables, too.

Not that he was interested in hearing how much she admired his work, she thought wistfully as she tugged the other sock on. He barely talked to her.

Most of all, though, Flynn had managed not to touch her. Or let her touch him. She remembered the way his breath had felt, warm and moist on her lips, sighed, then pushed the memory away. As she had done, over and over, every night for the past two weeks.

Emma's sneakers sat side by side two feet away. She contemplated them for a moment, and considered going barefoot to the appointment with her new gynecologist. Retrieving things from the floor was getting tricky.

But there were ways around most problems.

She used her toe to shimmy first one sneaker, then the other, close enough that she could lean sideways and pick them up. Then she did the foot-on-knee thing again so she could pull them on and tie them.

The problem of Flynn's skittishness could be dealt with, too. Not comfortably, maybe, but she knew what she needed to do. She'd tried to let him know by her actions that he didn't have anything to worry about, but that didn't seem to be working.

Poor man. Her face heated with embarrassment. He shouldn't have to suffer for her out-of-whack hormones. And she shouldn't have to live with someone who acted as if she had a contagious disease.

Emma stood and smoothed the silky rayon of her newest maternity top. It was a rich, deep blue, with fussy little buttons down the front and pleats that lay flat across her breasts, then spread into gathers at the swell of her belly.

A woman's ego was a funny thing, she reflected wryly. She'd pulled out her hot rollers this morning in an effort to tame her curls into some sort of style. She'd even fussed with some of the makeup Miranda had given her. It was silly, she supposed, to shore up her ego by fussing with her clothes and hair when she was planning on flattening it once she got in the car with Flynn. But so what? Whatever works, she told herself—and barely resisted the urge to add a spritz of cologne to her preparations.

She didn't want to alarm the poor man. He could easily misinterpret her need to feel pretty today, and that would mess up her plans.

There was a knock on her door. "You ready?" Flynn called. "It's a twenty-minute drive to Burnet, and your appointment is in thirty minutes."

"I'll be right out."

Emma grabbed her purse, then was halted by the mirror that hung on the back of the door. It showed her a smiling woman whose brown hair was a careful tumble of curls—and whose stomach was hugely, obviously pregnant. Her mood took a sudden nosedive.

Maybe she had been hoping, just a little, that Flynn would think she was pretty. And maybe, if it had been his baby she was carrying instead of...

No, she was not going there. Not even for a second.

* * *

The Texas Hill Country was vastly different from Arizona or southern California. The land dipped and curved, bumping itself up into hills, pausing to stretch out here and there in a cheerfully haphazard way. And it was all so green. Everywhere Emma looked, green was growing its way up, in one shape of leaf or another, toward the sun.

Then there were the wildflowers. She smiled as they passed a tiny meadow drenched in Texas bluebonnets. Wildflowers grew everywhere, popping out as liberally as freckles on a redhead.

Fairytale country, she thought dreamily. Whimsical and cozy, full of flowers and quiet secrets. It lacked only a castle or two.

"You've hardly said a word since you got in the car," Flynn said. "What's on your mind?"

"Castles." And putting off the evil moment. "Have you ever been to Europe?"

"I was stationed in Germany for awhile when I was in the Army. Why?"

"You were in the Army?' She sat up straighter. "And stationed in Germany? Oh, that must have been wonderful. I thought about enlisting at one time."

Flynn tried to picture the pixie beside him wearing fatigues, with an M-14 rifle slung over her shoulder. He snorted. "Somehow I don't see you as the combat boot type. Tofu and channeling, yeah. Forced marches, no. What changed your mind? The thought of all those nasty guns?"

"I decided the Army and I wouldn't be philosophically compatible." She shot him a mischievous smile. "I'll bet you had the same problem. People who enjoy giving orders as much as you do seldom want to take them."

"Actually, for awhile I thought I'd make a career of it."

"You did?" Her eyebrows made twin arcs of surprise. "What changed your mind?"

"My dad died when I was twenty."

"Oh, I'm sorry." She laid her hand on his arm.

"It was a long time ago. Sixteen years." Why had he even brought it up? He frowned.

"Time helps." She nodded as if she'd learned that the hard way. "But when we lose someone important, the ache never goes away completely. Why did you have to leave the army?"

He shrugged, uncomfortable with the subject he'd brought up himself. "My stepmom needed me. Stella's great, don't get me wrong, but she'd never so much as balanced a checkbook in her life. No way could she have run or disposed of a business." Especially one in the shape his father's construction company had been in when he died. Lord, that had come as a shock. If Kingston Fortune hadn't offered a long-term, low-interest loan to the son of his old college buddy, the company would have ended up bankrupt. Flynn had had to run the business himself for a while, but he'd hated it. Eventually he had hired a manager to handle the firm. "She was lost without Dad. Then there were my sisters."

"You have sisters?" She sounded excited.

"Carrie and Joy. They're my stepsisters, technically, but family is family." He changed the subject before she could ask any more questions. "I can't imagine you in the army. Why did you even consider it?"

"Oh, for the chance to travel. To see Europe, especially." She got that dreamy look on her face again. "Does it look anything like this? All the hills, everything green, the little towns snuggled up like sleepy puppies?"

"I guess so. A lot of the Germans who landed in Texas thought the Hill Country looked like home, and settled here." It occurred to him that soon Emma would be able to travel all she wanted. For some reason, the idea made him tense. "Will you go to Europe after the baby's born?"

She laughed. "Oh, sure. I look like I can afford to tour Europe, don't I?"

Puzzled, he glanced at her. "Once your mother's lawyers finish playing with the whereases and whatfors, you'll be able to go anywhere you damned well please."

"Oh. That." She shot him a cheeky grin. "I'm just hoping I'll have enough left after paying your bill to set up a college fund for the baby."

"My bill will be a nice chunk of change," he said dryly, "but I think you'll have some left."

"Good." She looked out the window again, her lips curving up. "You know, I didn't like the idea at first. Of taking money from Miranda, I mean."

"I noticed."

"But the more I think about it, the more I see that was foolish. Sure, I'd rather do everything myself. But even after I set aside a goodly portion for college and pay your bill, there will be some left to invest for the baby. At first I thought that's what I would do with it—tuck it away, not touch it. But that was selfish."

Not to mention half-crazy, considering how much money they were talking about. "So you've decided to quit bitching about the money?"

She nodded. "Whatever doesn't go towards a college fund can be invested to provide some extra income. I don't know much about that, but I can learn. There are a lot of things I'd have trouble affording on my own, you know? A few hundred dollars a month would pay for a lot of extras for Angie." She rubbed her stomach lovingly. "Like ballet lessons, or a horse."

A few hundred a month? He shot her an incredulous look.

"Or band," she added. "That can get expensive. Even the secondhand instruments aren't cheap. Then there are special trips, private lessons, repairs…did you know that a box of reeds costs more than thirty dollars?" She shook her head, appalled.

"I take it you were in band." He didn't know how much money Miranda planned to settle on her daughter, but he had some idea of how much money the Fortunes had.

Emma was expecting a few hundred dollars a month?

"Saxophone, in the seventh and eighth grade." She grinned. "I was awful. Great rhythm, lousy embouchure. I squeaked every time I tried to hit high C."

"Maybe you should have tried drums instead of the sax." If Miranda settled only a small portion of what she'd inherited on Emma—say, a tenth or less—and Emma invested it conservatively…

"Do you know how much drums *cost?*"

"Not really." A couple thousand, he thought. That's what her income might be, after taxes. But that was a couple thousand a *day,* not a month. And that was the minimum. It might be a lot more.

She told him a funny story about her days in band before she decided she wasn't cut out to be a musician. At least, that was the reason she gave for dropping band, but Flynn could read between the lines. She'd loved it. If there had been money for what she called the extras, or for that set of drums she'd secretly lusted after, she would have stayed.

He managed to respond to her cheerful chatter, but all he could think was, *she hasn't got a clue.* She really had no idea how much money was coming her way.

Another woman would be thrilled to learn she was going to be stinking rich. Another woman, having done without even the little luxuries all her life, would be over the moon to learn she'd soon be counting her pocket change in the thousands of dollars instead of pennies and dimes.

Not Emma. She was going to hate it. The fact that she hadn't earned the money would make her crazy, striking hard at her cherished independence. Then, too, real money—big money—built fences. It would change her entire life, isolate her from the kind of people she'd always known. And for Emma, that kind of money would carry tremendous responsibility. It would be more burden than prize.

Then there was the fact that the money was coming to her from the woman she refused to call mother.

"Of course," she was saying, "John may not have any interest in being in the band. I wonder what he'll be like?" One hand spread over her stomach in a gesture as loving as it was unconscious. "I'm getting eager to meet him and find out."

Her face had that glow again, the one that made no sense. He looked for the shadows that had to be there, the hauntings left by a childhood spent in borrowed homes where there wasn't enough of anything to go around. Later shadows, cast by memories of blows and fear.

He didn't see them. It wasn't the first time he'd looked and failed to see what had to be there. Most of the time she glowed, as if life burned too quick and bright in her for shadows to linger. But he'd seen her dark places once. When she'd talked about Steven Shaw.

He kept his tone light. "So the baby is John now? Last I heard, it was Abigail. Or was it Annie?"

"I haven't found the right name yet. I keep trying them out, waiting for one to feel right. Is that Burnet up ahead?"

"Yeah. There's not a lot of it, but at least there's a hospital." When he'd arranged to bring her to his cabin, he'd thought vaguely that it was a good thing there was a hospital nearby, just in case. Now he was beginning to worry. It was a small hospital, without the kind of up-to-date equipment she would have had available in San Antonio.

What if something went wrong?

His fingers tightened on the steering wheel. "You like the sound of this doctor you're seeing today?"

"Since he's the only gynecologist in town, I'd better." She glanced at him. "Hey, relax. According to his nurse, Dr. Howell has been delivering babies for thirty years, and Kane speaks highly of him. I'll admit I would rather have had a midwife—"

"A midwife?" He had visions of some wrinkled old crone giving her a strap to chew on. "What the hell kind of idea is that?"

"A popular one, in lots of places. If I'd stayed in San Diego…" Her voice trailed off. "Well, that wasn't possible. At least Dr. Howell isn't one of those old-fashioned physicians who think they're supposed to be in charge of the birthing, instead of the mother. His nurse said he was responsible for the hospital getting a birthing chair."

Apparently she thought that was a good thing. Flynn wasn't sure what a birthing chair was, but the images it conjured made him uneasy.

They'd reached Burnet, and he slowed to the posted speed limit. "You don't have to use this doctor if you don't want to. Burnet's close, but so is Johnson City. Shoot, Austin is only forty minutes away, though once we hit the city limit, traffic can be a bitch. If you were in a hurry…" He thought about having to make an emergency trip to Austin, and swallowed.

With luck, he reminded himself, Shaw would be out of the picture before her baby decided to show up. She could go back to San Antonio and stay with her mother, who knew about having babies.

"I'm sure Dr. Howell will be fine."

"You're doing all right," he informed her, unease ripening into worry. "You haven't been sick in the mornings. Although you do sleep a lot…" What had he been thinking when he brought her to the cabin? He didn't know anything about taking care of a pregnant woman. Worry roughened his voice. "You took two naps yesterday."

"I nap a lot because I wake up a lot to pop in and out of the bathroom. You must have noticed that." Her smile was easy and unembarrassed.

He'd noticed. They'd modified their original agreement concerning the bathroom. After bedtime, it was all hers.

She smiled and laid her hand on his shoulder. "Honest, Flynn, I'm fine."

One touch. That's all it took to have him heating, wanting more. He stiffened and pulled away.

Six

Emma dropped her hand. The moment she'd been dreading had come. Flynn had given her the perfect opening.

She smiled brightly. "Lots of things are normal for a pregnant woman that might seem alarming. Like morning sickness. Not every woman experiences it, but it's entirely normal in the first trimester or so."

"Did you have morning sickness?"

"No, I'm happy to say I missed that. The doctor I saw in Arizona said I was made for having babies. He was nuts about my pelvic bones."

Flynn turned into a parking lot alongside a trim single-story house that had been converted into offices. "I don't think I want to know what your pelvic bones have to do with anything."

"If you're a good boy, I won't tell you."

"Fine." He pulled to a stop without cutting off the engine. "How long do you think this will take? I thought I'd run some errands and come back for you."

"An hour, maybe." She took a deep breath. It was now or never, and never was unacceptable. "Lots of things are normal for a pregnant woman, Flynn, that may seem strange to you. Like morning sickness and backaches and rampaging hormones."

His quick glance was a hard green several shades brighter than the polo shirt he wore beneath a lightweight jacket. "Sounds like another thing I don't really need to know."

"Maybe you do, though. Since we're living together. Out-of-whack hormones can mean out-of-whack emotions. I've cried over commercials. That one with the little boy and the ducks…" She shook her head and unclicked her seat belt. "Gets me every time."

He eyed her warily. "Do radio commercials jerk your tear ducts, too?"

"No, but there are a couple of country-western songs that ought to have a warning label. The thing is, weepiness is entirely normal, and it doesn't mean anything is wrong." She took a deep breath and plunged ahead. "Then there's sex."

The dead silence in the car told her she had his full attention.

"Some women experience heightened sexual feelings during pregnancy," she said matter-of-factly as if her cheeks weren't hot enough to set off a smoke alarm. "Again, it doesn't mean anything, except that we might be a little off-balance, hormonally. In case you haven't figured it out," she added, turning to him with a reassuring smile, "I'm trying to tell you that you don't have to work so hard at avoiding me. I'm not going to pounce on you."

"Uh…"

"I know I embarrassed you the other day, and I'm sorry for it. But you don't have to be concerned about giving me the wrong idea. My hormones may be a little topsy-turvy

these days, but my common sense is still working fine."
She chuckled. "So's my mirror."

So far, her campaign to put him at ease didn't seem to
be working. He was rubbing his temple as if he had a head-
ache. "You think I'm avoiding you because I'm embarrassed."

"It's perfectly understandable. You're a kind man. You
don't know me well enough to realize I'm not going to
mistake that kindness for something else."

"So I'm kind. And sweet? I think you said that once.
And you're…what?" Slowly he turned his head, and confused her utterly. His jaw was hard and his narrowed eyes
were ablaze with all the wrong feelings. Feelings that
made sparks dance along her spine. "An idiot? A crazy
woman?"

"Ah—Flynn?" Those sparks zipped through her system,
fizzing her brain and shooting out invisibly to mess up the
air, which turned thick and exotic in her lungs. "You aren't
taking this the way I'd expected."

"Emma." His fingers drummed on the steering wheel.
"This may have escaped your attention, but I am not pregnant."

"I was pretty sure you weren't." Meeting those glinting
green eyes became impossible, but when she looked away
her attention was snagged by his arm. The cuff of his jacket
was unsnapped and the sleeve was rolled up, leaving his
forearm bare, exposed to the weirdly thickened air and her
lascivious attention.

"There's nothing wrong with my hormones."

"No, of course not." Fascinated, she watched the muscles flex in that arm as he released the steering wheel…and
reached for her.

He closed his hand around her arm. "You want to know
what you are? A woman with no better sense than to trust

a man she barely knows. It's been driving me crazy, and it's going to stop, right now.''

To prove his point, he pulled her closer. Or maybe she leaned into the kiss—she didn't know, couldn't tell, which of them closed the distance. But she knew the second that distance was gone, and his mouth was on hers.

He didn't crush or tease or coerce. He compelled. With the drift of his lips across hers, with the faint, musky scent of man and soap, with the sunlight falling warm and fluid over them both.

"A woman," he murmured, "who has no idea how lovely she is. How incredibly sexy…" He punctuated his words with brief, nibbling kisses, kisses that spoke silently of a wealth of tenderness spiced by need. "A woman with the stupid idea that men won't be turned on by her rounded body. Really dumb, Emma." Another kiss, with a taste of tongue that had her clutching at his wonderfully bare forearms. "Think about all those primitive tribes whose goddesses were round, sexy, pregnant…"

Think? He wanted her to think, when her hand had found its way to his chest, where his heart raced just the way hers was? How could she think? Dreams welled in the air, heady and shapeless and strong, drawing her to the promise of his body and the sweetness of his mouth.

His hand slid up the swell of her breast, and it felt so natural, so right. When he rubbed the peak, a jolt of pure heat sent her head spinning.

She needed to be closer to him, as close as she could get. Emma reached for the nape of his neck where the skin was deliciously rough. She opened her mouth to his and slid her other hand beneath his jacket—and encountered a shoulder holster. With a gun in it.

Before she'd finished processing that fact, he jerked his head back. His eyes were wide and alarmed. He dropped his hand.

Dizzy, confused, she searched his face. "Flynn—?"

"You'll be late." His eyes were hard now. His breathing wasn't steady. "You'd better go in." He took her hand from his neck and then looked at it as if he had no idea how it came to be held in his. "That won't happen again. But now you know."

He threw open the door and got out, apparently convinced he had explained himself. And Emma sat in the musty warmth of the car, still tasting him and the bright, impossible promises that flowed through her, fragile and shiny as soap bubbles. Sat there while those promises popped, one by one, as dreams always do.

He had wanted to kiss her. But he didn't like wanting her, and he didn't want anything more than a single kiss.

When she collected her purse and climbed out of the car, he was waiting. "Don't worry," she said once more as she blinked away the dampness tangled in her eyelashes that was trying to turn ordinary sunlight into rainbows. "I understand now. You're not kind at all."

"Will she file charges?" Ryan Fortune asked. "She left the state because she didn't trust the police."

Flynn sat in his car with the cell phone cradled to his ear and frowned at the door to the doctor's office. "I think she will, if she doesn't have to go back to California to do it."

"I didn't know it was possible to press charges from outside the jurisdiction where the assault took place."

"Usually it isn't. But with your money paying for an investigation and the help of the sheriff's office here, it can be done."

"You haven't said anything to Emma about all this?"

"I wanted to get the loose ends tied up first."

Ryan Fortune had called Flynn the day after he brought Emma to the lake. The man would make a fine old-time patriarch, Flynn thought; he wouldn't stand for anyone threatening a member of his family. He wanted Shaw put away quickly, and for a nice, long time.

Flynn agreed. The two men had come to terms readily.

"Let me know when you've finished tying knots," Ryan said. "I'm more than ready to hear that Shaw is behind bars."

"He'll make bail," Flynn cautioned him. "And if Emma won't go back to testify, there's not much chance of a conviction."

"But with this hanging over him, he won't be able to leave the state. Not if he wants to keep his license."

"That's the idea." Flynn switched subjects. "I guess you haven't heard from Holly Douglas." That young woman was the only one of the lost Fortune heirs he'd tracked down who hadn't attended the party at the ranch. She lived in Alaska, so he'd let someone else handle the contact. That had probably been a mistake. She'd turned down the invitation cold. Apparently there was another Fortune who was less than thrilled by her newfound connection.

"I said I'd call if she turned up," Ryan snapped.

Flynn's eyebrows rose. "Good enough."

"Sorry. I've been fighting a stomach bug…yes, Lily, what is it?" His voice faded, as if he'd turned away from the phone. Flynn faintly heard Ryan's wife in the background. "No, food probably isn't a good idea. Maybe later…don't fuss. I'm fine." His voice grew distinct again. "I take it Emma's doing okay? No complications?"

Not unless you counted the fact that the man who was supposed to be protecting her had been ready to pull her clothes off in the car an hour ago. "She says she's fine. She doesn't look swollen or anything."

There was a moment's silence, then a low chuckle. "If you haven't noticed the swelling, you're not as observant as I thought."

"I meant in her hands and feet, like happens with that toxemia stuff." Before calling Ryan, Flynn had gone to the library and scared himself silly. He'd had no idea so many things could go wrong with a pregnancy.

"Sounds like you've been doing your homework." There was sympathy as well as amusement in Ryan's voice.

"I thought I should know what I'm dealing with. I'll be in touch when—hell, here she comes." Flynn said goodbye and disconnected.

What had he been thinking of, making himself responsible for a woman in Emma's condition? Obviously, he *hadn't* been thinking. It wasn't like him to act on impulse, but that's what he'd done. Now he had to live with the consequences.

The chief consequence was nearly to the car, her curls bobbing cheerfully, her briefcase-size purse tucked beneath one arm. He checked out her hands and feet. They didn't look swollen, but who could tell when she wore athletic shoes? Terms like *intrauterine-growth retardation, pre-eclampsia, placental abruption,* and *polyhydramnios* swam through his head while he reached across and shoved open the passenger door.

"Hi!" She slid inside. "I was wondering if we could do some shopping before we head back to the cabin."

Apparently they were gong to pretend he hadn't lost what remained of his mind and kissed her. Fine. "So what did the doctor say?"

She pulled the seat belt across, adjusting the strap so it didn't compress her tummy. "The big picture is, I'm in great shape."

"Maybe you could be a little more specific." He thought of some of the things he'd read. "Your blood pressure okay?"

"One-eleven over sixty-eight."

"How about your iron?"

"It's fine."

"Any sugar in your urine?"

A laugh sputtered out. "I can't believe you asked about my urine."

He couldn't, either. "I, uh, did some reading. Women over thirty-five are twice as likely to have complications with pregnancy-induced diabetes. Of course, you're not thirty-five yet—"

"I'm not diabetic, either. Or anemic. Dr. Howell agrees with my doctor in Arizona. I'm good at baby-making."

He didn't say anything while he reversed, shifted, and pulled up to the exit. "What kind of shopping do you need to do? There's a supermarket up ahead."

"I was thinking more of garage sales." She pulled a folded sheet of newspaper from her purse. "I thought it was time to get a crib. Why are you wearing a gun?"

"Why do you think?" A crib. God. That sounded so...definite. There was a baby, an actual baby, inside her. "I'm supposed to be protecting you. Why do you want a used crib? Don't tell me you can't afford a new one."

"I can't afford anything! Miranda is paying for it all— the doctor, the hospital, everything. She's giving me an *allowance*." She spat that word out the way Flynn used to spit out spinach when he was a kid. "I was doing okay on my own. I'd prepaid half the doctor and hospital bill before you found me. I didn't dare stay there long enough to get my money back, and I sure couldn't have them send it to me—if my address was in their system, Steven might get it. Now I don't have anything that doesn't come from her."

"She's your mother. And she can afford it."

"I know." Her fingers were twisting the strap of her purse. "But I thought...if I buy a used crib and paint it or refinish it myself, it will be more from me, not just something Miranda's money paid for."

FREE GIFTS!

NO COST! NO OBLIGATION TO BUY!
NO PURCHASE NECESSARY!

PLAY THE
Lucky Key Game

Scratch gold area with a coin.
Then check below to see the gifts you get!

326 SDL DC64
225 SDL DC6Y

YES! I have scratched off the gold area. Please send me the 2 Free books and gift for which I qualify. I understand I am under no obligation to purchase any books, as explained on the back and on the opposite page.

NAME   (PLEASE PRINT CLEARLY)

ADDRESS

APT.#   CITY

STATE/PROV.   ZIP/POSTAL CODE

2 free books plus a mystery gift   1 free book

2 free books   Try Again!

Offer limited to one per household and not valid to current Silhouette Desire® subscribers. All orders subject to approval.

(S-D-OS-07/01)

The Silhouette Reader Service™ — Here's how it works:

Accepting your 2 free books and gift places you under no obligation to buy anything. You may keep the books and gift and return the shipping statement marked "cancel." If you do not cancel, about a month later we'll send you 6 additional novels and bill you just $3.34 each in the U.S., or $3.74 each in Canada, plus 25¢ shipping & handling per book and applicable taxes if any.* That's the complete price and — compared to cover prices of $3.99 each in the U.S. and $4.50 each in Canada — it's quite a bargain! You may cancel at any time, but if you choose to continue, every month we'll send you 6 more books, which you may either purchase at the discount price or return to us and cancel your subscription.

*Terms and prices subject to change without notice. Sales tax applicable in N.Y. Canadian residents will be charged applicable provincial taxes and GST.

If offer card is missing write to: Silhouette Reader Service, 3010 Walden Ave., P.O. Box 1867, Buffalo, NY 14240-1867

BUSINESS REPLY MAIL

FIRST-CLASS MAIL   PERMIT NO. 717-003   BUFFALO, NY

POSTAGE WILL BE PAID BY ADDRESSEE

SILHOUETTE READER SERVICE
3010 WALDEN AVE
PO BOX 1867
BUFFALO NY 14240-9952

NO POSTAGE
NECESSARY
IF MAILED
IN THE
UNITED STATES

He nodded. "Is it okay for you to mess with paint and solvents?"

"As long as there's good ventilation."

"The back porch is screened," he said, pulling into the parking lot at the grocery store. "Excellent ventilation. That's why I work out there. I could refinish the crib for you. I'd enjoy it."

She stopped mutilating her purse. "I wouldn't mind some help. You know a lot more about wood than I do. But I need something to do, and I like the idea of working on it myself." She glanced around. "Maybe we should pick up the groceries last, after we've found the crib."

"I pulled in here so I could see where we're going." He reached for the folded sheet of newspaper.

She held it out. Their fingers brushed. Her hand zipped back so fast the paper fluttered to the seat before he could grab it. She licked her lips. "I, uh, circled the ones that looked promising."

Anger and frustration burst from him. "I shouldn't have done it, all right?"

Her eyes went wide.

"I told myself I was doing it for your own good. That I was going to kiss all those stupid ideas about being undesirable out of your head. But that wasn't true." Guilt rumbled in, making his voice lower. "I kissed you because I wanted to. You were right. I wasn't being kind."

She didn't say anything, just stared at him as if he'd grown a new nose.

"Dammit." He scrubbed a hand over the top of his head and tried not to think about one of the books he'd read at the library—*Dr. Ruth's Pregnancy Guide for Couples.* Images of some of the recommended positions kept trying to float across his mental landscape. "Do you want me to apologize?"

She looked down and picked up the newspaper. "I think

you just did, in a backhanded, annoyingly male sort of way. It's okay, Flynn.''

''I'll keep my hands to myself from now on.''

She nodded, her head still down. ''There's a place on Glenwood that mentions baby furniture. Do you know where that is?''

''Yeah.'' He dragged in a deep breath and let it out in a sigh. ''The thing is, Emma, I'm a pretty shallow guy when it comes to relationships. I like to keep things casual. No strings.''

Now she looked up, her eyes the deep, impenetrable blue of the lake when it was calm. ''I see. Light and loose and fun for both parties?''

''That's right.'' She understood. Relief eased the tension in his shoulders. ''And you can't be interested in that sort of thing. You need someone who's going to stick around, take care of you and the baby.''

''But I'm very interested in you, Flynn. And I can take care of myself.''

Oh, hell. He slammed the car into gear. ''What kind of crib are we looking for?''

He'd wanted her. Yesterday, Flynn Sinclair had definitely wanted her. That thought kept singing in Emma's mind, even while part of her chuckled over a story Flynn was telling her about his army days.

At least it hadn't been a pity kiss. She'd wondered. He'd looked so appalled to find his arms full of melting, wanting, oh-so-pregnant woman.

He'd been alarmed, all right. But it was his response that had shaken him, not hers. She was sure of that. Well— almost sure, she amended with scrupulous mental honesty as she smoothed her sandpaper along a crib rail. Even if she'd mistaken his motives, though, she knew he'd wanted her.

Emma hummed as she buffed out a rough spot. She was over her hurt, which had been pretty pointless. Of course he wasn't looking to get tangled up with her. But a woman could still be pleased to learn that she was wanted by the man she was falling in love with. Even if neither of them intended to do anything about it.

She wasn't sure exactly when she'd known she was falling for Flynn. By the time he kissed her, it seemed as if she'd already known it for some time. She just hadn't been paying attention.

He didn't feel the same way. He'd been making that clear in a dozen ways since yesterday—as if she'd needed the hint. She shook her head and reached for a sheet of fine-grade sandpaper as Flynn finished a story involving a fish, a corporal and a wet-behind-his-ears second lieutenant.

She grinned. "If half the tales you've told me are true, your superior officers must have been praying you wouldn't reenlist."

"Rumor has it that the captain held a private celebration the day I left."

She'd been coaxing stories from him while they worked on the lovely old Jenny Lind crib she'd bought yesterday. Disassembled pieces of that crib lay scattered around them on the back porch. Years ago, someone had painted it a violent shade of yellow. The paint was peeling in places and ugly all over, but the wood was sound, except for the footboard, which had been warped by damp. Flynn had insisted he'd enjoy replacing the damaged portion.

Having watched him play with wood all week, she believed him. "The captain didn't appreciate your sense of humor?"

"I can't say I blame him." He made an adjustment to the vise that clamped the footboard. "I was a definite pain in the ass. Thought I knew everything. Who doesn't, at that age?"

"How old were you?"

"The ink was almost dry on my high school diploma when I signed up."

"So you were still a kid when you pulled all these hi-jinks." The stories he'd told her had been funny, not terribly personal, and underlined what a wild, rootless soul he was. She'd gotten his point.

He drew a plane slowly along the length of wood. "Kids are always in a hurry. I couldn't wait to be out on my own, out from under my father's thumb. He wanted me to work for him at his construction firm. Naturally, that made me head for the other side of the world."

"I was like that, too." She ran her fingers over the wood. "Wild to be out on my own. I worked the fountain at the local drugstore all through high school, and saved every penny I could." She smiled, remembering. "Two days after graduation I had my car packed with all my worldly possessions. Me and Phil Collins sang 'True Colors' at the top of our lungs while I watched Dry Creek get smaller and smaller in my rearview mirror."

"Didn't like small town life?"

"Didn't like Dry Creek." She made a face. "I didn't fit in. I wanted to be a hippie."

He laughed. He had a surprising laugh, deep and sudden as thunder on a sunny day. She felt it deep inside her, stirring in hidden places. "You were a couple of decades too late for that, weren't you?"

"Yes, and it was one of the major sorrows of my teenage life. You have any idea how hard it was to get tie-dyed T-shirts in the eighties? Or anything with a peace symbol?"

"I can't say I ever tried. Why did you want to be a hippie?"

"Maybe because no one else did. And I always figured..." She stopped, knelt and attacked the bottom runner with her sandpaper. "This is just about ready, I think."

"You wondered if your mother had been a hippie."

She shrugged. "I guess. I was born in '69, right at the end of the peace-and-love era." For so many years Emma had carried a picture in her mind of the woman her mother might have been—young, a little lost. A little sad. A flower child who'd found herself in Dry Creek, Nevada, with a baby she couldn't take care of. "For some reason I always thought she came from California. San Francisco, maybe, because of the song." She found a smile. "You know—the one about going to San Francisco and finding some gentle people there. I pictured a real California girl—tan and skinny and blond, with blue eyes." Like Emma's.

Miranda had come from Texas, not California, and she'd left her babies because she didn't want to go home and let her family know how badly she'd messed up.

But she had been terribly young. That much of Emma's picture had been true.

"Dry Creek isn't far from the California border."

"No, and the one thing I knew about her was that she wasn't local. Mama Jo told me that."

"Mama Jo?"

"She was my second foster mother." Flakes of paint scattered as she rubbed the old wood. "Her name was really Jo Ann Weathers—Mrs. Dan Weathers—but everyone called them Mama Jo and Papa Dan."

"Was she the one who wanted to adopt you?"

"Yeah." She sighed, remembering. "When Papa Dan got transferred, they wanted to take me with them. It didn't work out."

"That must have been rough."

"At least I knew they wanted me."

He was silent a moment. "Miranda isn't much like the mother you'd imagined, is she?"

Emma rubbed harder with the sandpaper. "I never thought she was from Texas, that's for sure. Or that she might be rich.'' Poor little rich girl, got in trouble and ran away from home, then left her babies on a handy doorstep. "Maybe it shouldn't make any difference, but it does. She could have kept us. She had money. She was just pretending she didn't.''

"The line between pride and pretense can be hard to spot sometimes," he agreed mildly. "Especially when you're seventeen. You might want to take it easy on the sanding. If you keep rubbing that hard, you're going to sand right through the rail, if your arm doesn't fall off first.''

Emma blinked. Sawdust and paint flakes were flying, her fingers were cramping and her arm ached. She stopped. "I could use a drink. You want something?''

"Sure.''

She started to go through the usual preparations it took to get to her feet these days. Flynn was on his feet before she could rise, holding out a hand. She hesitated, then took it. His palm was warm and calloused, and she could have gone on holding it for an hour or two. Reluctantly she let go and rubbed the small of her back, where an ache competed with the one in her arm.

"Your back hurting?''

"Just tired.'' She started for the doorway.

"You never went back to Dry Creek, did you?''

She paused. "No, I didn't, but how did you know that?''

"I went to Dry Creek at one point when I was looking for you. Thought you might have kept in touch with someone. Plenty of people remembered you, but no one had seen you since high school.'' He put the plane down and picked up a level. "By the way, a couple of your teachers gave me messages for you. I should have passed them on before now.''

Memory twisted inside, a happy-sad burst like biting into a lemon drop. "Mr. Adamson?''

"He said to tell you it's never too late. You can still give college a try."

She smiled. She'd liked her art teacher. He'd liked her, too, though he'd been frustrated by her lack of ambition. "Who else?"

"Mrs. Jordan."

"My English teacher?" That surprised her. "I nearly flunked her class. Twice." Jefferson High was a small school. Mrs. Jordan had been one of only two English teachers, and Emma had ended up having her every year.

"She said you were a remarkably bright young lady who would do well once you understood that rules and creativity weren't necessarily antithetical."

"Antithetical." She grinned. "That sounds like Mrs. Jordan. She was as big on vocabulary as she was on rules." It warmed her to think that Mrs. Jordan had remembered her. "She must be retired by now."

"No, she's still teaching. The principal—a skinny man with big ears named John McIntyre—said she refuses to leave."

"Johnny McIntyre is the principal?" That was the biggest surprise yet. "I can't picture it. He skipped school more often than I did."

"I guess he shows up pretty regularly now."

They shared a grin. His expression changed, softened. "Why have you never been back, Emma?"

"Life is meant to be lived forward, not backward."

"But you carry the past with you. We all do." He picked up the plane again and drew it along the wood in one slow, careful stroke. "You went to see your Mama Jo when you left Dry Creek."

Her mouth drew down. "I thought you didn't know who she was."

"I knew who Jo Ann Weathers was, and where she went

when she left Dry Creek. I didn't know she was the foster mother who'd wanted to adopt you.''

''I don't like you knowing things about me that I haven't told you.''

''I'm a nosy man,'' he said mildly. ''That's why detective work suits me. You didn't abandon all of your past, did you? You stayed in touch with Jo and Dan Weathers.'' His attention seemed wholly fixed on the motion of his hands as he drew the plane along the wood again, smoothing it. Making things even. ''When Dan Weathers died, you went to the funeral. A year later, you quit your job in Phoenix so you could stay with Jo Weathers, because she was dying, too.''

She turned abruptly and headed for the kitchen.

Seven

Emma didn't pour herself a drink right away. Her hands were shaking too badly.

Falling for the man was one thing. Letting him connect with the private, tucked-away places in her life was something altogether different. She didn't like it. Flynn had visited Jefferson High, maybe hung around the drugstore, asking people if they remembered her. He'd found out about Mama Jo and the time Emma had spent nursing her.

She really didn't like that. It went too deep. Emma's eyes squeezed shut.

No one stays. No one ever, ever stays. Even Mama Jo and Papa Dan had left her...and she, in turn, had left them.

Mama Jo had been alone after Papa Dan's death. She'd needed Emma. Sure, she'd told Emma she was fine, not to worry, to go on with her life. That had been just like her. Emma should have known better. But all she had been able to think about was getting away, as if she could leave her

grief behind on the highway. And a year later, Mama Jo
had been diagnosed with a fast-growing cancer.

That time Emma had stayed. For two months, she'd held
Mama Jo's hand and washed her, listened to her and lost
her, one day at a time. She'd been there when Mama Jo
died, but she hadn't been around to share the living.

Emma closed her eyes, letting the pain and guilt slide
through her. If there was one thing she'd learned in the
terrible days of Mama Jo's dying, it was that she couldn't
fight her feelings any better than she could run away from
them. All she could do was ride them out.

Like she was going to have to ride out these feelings she
had for Flynn.

She took a deep, cleansing breath and went to the refrigerator. Her hands were steady when she poured a glass of
juice.

Falling in love was easy. How many times had she taken
that dizzy plunge? Emma always fell in love quickly…and
she fell out again just as fast. Mama Jo had told her once
that she was in love with the idea of love. She'd probably
been right. Emma enjoyed the whole, dizzy business, the
shivers and longing, the way hot and cold could flash
through her system at the same time. She knew the symp-
toms, and she knew they would run their course in time.

Rather like a head cold, she thought, sipping the tangy
juice. Or the flu. Sooner or later, her attraction for Flynn
would fade as surely as morning mist evaporates beneath
the steady climb of the sun.

It wasn't the way she wanted to be, wasn't the way she
wanted her life to be. But experience had taught her the
truth about herself.

There was something lacking in her. Maybe it was ge-
netic, a flaw she'd inherited from her mother. Maybe she'd
never learned how to connect in a permanent way. The
experts said there were key stages in an infant's life when

the need to bond with a single person was vital to the child's development. Maybe she'd missed one or more of those bonding times. No one had stayed with her, so she didn't know how to stick it out, either.

Whatever the cause, Emma knew better than to expect the way she felt for Flynn to last. Look at how quickly her feelings for Steven had fizzled. Even before she found out she was pregnant and he went crazy on her…she shivered and shoved those memories aside.

She couldn't encourage Flynn. She couldn't allow the fizzy heat in her blood to pull her one inch closer than she could afford to go, for both their sakes.

The phone rang. She kept sipping her juice. Flynn would get it. She wasn't supposed to answer the silly thing, just in case someone called who shouldn't know she was here.

Sure enough, he came into the great room and picked up the cell phone. Sun slanting through the skylight hit him squarely, as if he'd been spotlighted on stage. He wore jeans and a dingy green T-shirt that looked like a relic from his army days. A bead of sweat trickled down his temple; his T-shirt clung damply in places. There was sawdust on his jeans to match the dust that danced in the beam of sunlight.

She wanted to lick his neck. That made her smile. And rub her chest, where her heart ached. Her smile faded.

Flynn thought he wanted only temporary relationships. He'd warned her outright, and he'd made his point again today with all those stories about what a hellraiser he'd been.

If Emma had believed him, she would have been in his bed already. Oh, she didn't think he'd lied. He believed what he'd said, but he was wrong. Flynn was a good man, a forever kind of man. He deserved everything a woman could give him. He didn't deserve a woman who would be wildly in love one day and checking out the horizon the next.

He glanced her way. Quickly, before he could see the longing in her eyes, she turned and put her glass in the sink.

A minute later, he came into the kitchen area. "That was Martin. He wants us to come over for fish tonight."

She got her smile ready before turning to face him. "Are you going to badger me into baking those brownies he mentioned?"

"I'll make the brownies. You might want to put together a salad or something to get your vegetable fix. Martin does fine as long as he's frying things, but frying is all he knows how to do. I let him handle dessert once. Have you ever eaten fried Hostess Twinkies?"

Laughter tugged at her more seductively than lust had a moment ago. "Can't say I have. You really know how to bake brownies?"

"Sugar," he drawled, "my brownies are so good they've been banned in three states."

He made her laugh, he made her lust—and he baked brownies, too? "You're a dangerous man, Flynn Sinclair."

"Damned straight."

"Think that wind's pushing a storm this way?" Flynn asked lazily.

The three of them sat out on Martin's deck, the one Flynn had helped build. Martin had been a demon for building and fixing and generally working until he dropped for a couple of years after his wife died.

"Could be." Martin sipped from a big mug that read Fishermen Do It With A Lure and made a satisfied sound. "Anyone want another brownie?"

"I would, but if I ate it you'd have to kill me to put me out of my misery." Emma leaned back in her chair, her feet propped up on a low table. "I can't believe I ate that much."

Behind the house, unseen, the sun was setting. To the north a flurry of darkened clouds piled up, chased by a wind that tasted of chilly heights where the air turns thin and violet. That wind chopped at the lake's surface, played with the branches of the elms and oaks, tangled itself up in Emma's hair and teased the hem of her skirt.

Flynn wished he could imitate the wind, in one or two ways. "You skimped on your vegetables tonight."

She patted her stomach. "A growing girl needs her protein. The catfish were delicious." She slid him a teasing glance. "The brownies weren't bad, either."

"You mean you didn't eat three of them just to be polite?"

She chuckled and closed her eyes, boneless and satisfied as a cat.

There was a glow to her. A trick of the light, he thought, or of her dress, which was as orange as the sunset. The gauzy material draped every swell of breast and belly in crinkled flame, while the declining daylight bathed her in hints of orange and gold. But some part of him was drawn to worship rather than to explain—the primitive, pagan reverence of a man for a breeding woman.

Beneath the thin material of her dress, her stomach moved—one smooth, rolling shift, like the swell of the ocean. And his breath caught.

The baby was moving. And he could *see* it. He swallowed. "Emma."

She opened her eyes and looked at him curiously.

"Your baby's moving."

"He does that a lot. Evenings, especially. I'm afraid he's going to be a night owl."

Flynn watched at the swell of her stomach, hoping to see that movement again. "He moves more in the evening?"

She nodded, curving her hand around the bottom of her stomach, gently rubbing. "Maybe he doesn't like the heat. He sure gets busy once it cools down."

"You're saying 'he.'"

She grinned. "I have to admit I'm more likely to say 'he' when my ribs are being used to practice karate kicks."

"Maybe *she's* working on ballet kicks."

"Maybe *he* is."

They shared a grin. She was all curves, he thought. From the narrow arch where wrist bent into forearm to the ripe mounds of her breasts, from the dreamy tilt of her eyes to the merry curve of her mouth, she was dainty and rounded and fascinating.

Their eyes met. Her grin faded. So did his.

She jerked her gaze away and slapped her arm. "Darn mosquitoes. I'd bite them back if I wasn't so full."

"Maybe we should go back inside," Martin said. "Got some business to discuss. Might be better to do it without fighting off the bloodsuckers."

Flynn's attention was yanked to Martin. He'd forgotten anyone else was there. He found Martin's eyes on him, curious and knowing, and felt exposed. "Yes, we do," he said slowly. He reminded himself that this woman was a client, but the label felt false and tight now that he'd held her. Kissed her.

He was paying for that mistake now. "I've got some news," he said.

Emma's boneless ease vanished in a subtle tightening of muscles. "What kind?"

"You remember that I told you I had some ideas about what to do about Shaw?"

"Oh, yeah. You wouldn't tell me anything."

"Not until I had things tied down a bit. With Martin's help—"

"Hey, I reckon I did more than help."

Flynn grinned and repeated, "With Martin's help, I've got it set up so you can press charges against Shaw for his assault without having to go back to California."

Her face went utterly still. "That's not possible. I—I asked the cops in Arizona…I didn't tell them who I was, but I asked them. I wanted to know if it was possible to file charges in one state for an assault that happened elsewhere. They said it didn't work that way."

"Normally that's true. You're pregnant and unable to travel, though. That makes a difference. So does the fact that Martin trained Pete Dobson back when he was a snot-nosed deputy. The result is that you can press charges here, and the sheriff's office will deal with the San Diego P.D. All you have to do is go into Marble Falls tomorrow and sign the complaint."

She pushed on the arms of her chair and stood. "No."

Flynn's eyebrows snapped down in a scowl. "Why the hell not?"

"Have you been in touch with the cops in San Diego?" she demanded. "Has this Sheriff Dobson contacted them already?"

"Pete's been in touch with them," Martin said. He hadn't moved. His hands were still laced over his big belly, but his eyes were sharply focused. "He had to, in order to set things up."

"Oh, God." She shoved at the air—a jerky, push-away motion. "Don't you see what you've done? He'll know. Steven will find out where I am. If he'd thought about leaving me alone, he won't now." Her eyes squeezed closed. "Now I've threatened him. He won't let me get away with it."

Flynn stood slowly. "Emma, give us some credit. Pete—Sheriff Dobson—made sure the San Diego officer handling the charges is aware that Shaw has friends on the force.

They'll keep it quiet. And the P.I. who has been putting together the evidence—''

''A P.I.?'' She rounded on him. ''You hired a private investigator without consulting me?''

''I handled it, but the man was hired by Ryan. The idea is to present the San Diego P.D. with a case clear enough that they can't afford not to act. He made sure the officer we took the case to wasn't one of Shaw's buddies, too.''

''I can't believe this.'' She dragged a hand through her hair. ''You had no right. You didn't consult me, you just charged ahead and did what you thought best.''

''Nothing's been done yet,'' he growled. ''If you refuse to press charges, nothing *will* be done. Shaw will still be free to leave the state and come after you—which he won't be, if he's been arrested.''

''Oh, that's reassuring.'' She gave a hard little laugh. ''Steven is so concerned with abiding by the law, after all. I'm sure he'll drop any idea of retaliating once he understands it could get him in trouble.''

''Emma.'' Martin spoke gently. ''You're scared, and you've got reason. The one thing Flynn and I couldn't be sure of is whether Shaw might hire someone.''

''Hire someone?'' She looked bewildered, then pale. ''Oh. You mean to—to come after me. No, he wouldn't do that.'' Her laugh was shaky. ''He'd probably be furious if I were hit by a car. There's no satisfaction if fate cheats him from winning on his own. He'd never leave revenge in someone else's hands.''

Flynn's hands clenched. It fit the profile they'd built of Shaw. It also made him want to put his fist through something.

Martin nodded. ''Then give the system a chance to work. Let the boys in blue get Shaw locked up.''

''He won't stay locked up, though, will he?'' She rubbed her forehead. ''I know you believe in the system, Martin.

I understand that. But your system can't offer me any guarantees, and I need them. I have to..." She looked away, swallowed. "If I sign that complaint, I'll have to leave. Maybe I should anyway."

A shock of fear jolted down Flynn's spine. "Is that your answer to everything? Running away?" He moved to her and closed his hands around her shoulders. "You think the monsters can't catch you if you stay on the move?"

Her eyes were glossy with tears and ghosts, all the ghosts he'd looked for before. Her voice was a whisper. "Can you promise that if I press charges against Steven, he won't be able to trace it here, to Marble Falls?"

No. No, he couldn't. Frustration tightened his fingers. "It's highly unlikely. That's the best I can do, Emma. Life doesn't come with a money-back guarantee. This is your best chance of stopping Shaw, and we've done everything possible to minimize the risk. If you won't take that chance, you're going to be running forever."

"If I do what you want, I'll still have to run."

"The hell you will. You're safer with me than heading off on your own."

"Is that your *professional* opinion?" Her light stress on the word made it a delicate mockery, conjuring heated memories.

He dropped his hands. "You've got a gift for sarcasm I hadn't suspected."

Martin heaved to his feet with a grunt. "Reckon I should let the two of you discuss this in private."

"No," Flynn said.

"Yes," Emma said at the same time. "Thank you, Martin."

Neither of them moved or spoke until the glass door slid shut behind him, sealing them outside in the gathering dusk. Then Emma turned away, facing the rail once more.

The wind tugged at her hair, dancing it around her face. "I like it here," she said wistfully. "Mosquitoes and all."

"That's good, because you're going to be here awhile. Leaving isn't an option until Shaw's locked up."

She sighed and turned. The glow he'd seen earlier was lost to the darkening air; only her eyes were luminous now. And sad, so sad. "Flynn, pressing charges against Steven isn't going to keep him in California. It will just infuriate him. He can't stand to be beaten, and that's how he'll see this—as a direct challenge."

"He'll be arrested. The case is tight."

"He'll be out on bail in less than twenty-four hours. And he'll come after me."

Feelings knotted up inside him, tight and complex. He wanted to take her tangled hair in his hands and smooth it, to ease the strain from her shoulders. He wanted to take her, period. "I'm not going to let him get to you."

"If Steven is really determined..." She wrapped her arms around herself. "You don't know what he's like. He's good, Flynn. He'll find me."

She had a lot more confidence in Shaw's ability to find her than she did in Flynn's ability to protect her. He told himself it didn't matter. "Okay, say he's nuts enough to ignore the terms of his bail. Say he's as brilliant as you claim, and he finds out the charges were filed in Texas. So he hops a plane and heads this way. The minute he crosses the state line..." He held his hand out, palm up—and slowly closed it. "We've got him."

"What do you mean? When I suggested setting a trap—"

"You wanted to act as bait. That's not happening." He'd resisted long enough. He stroked the hair back from her face that the wind had been messing with, and let his fingers linger on her cheek. "He's not going to get close to you, sugar. He'll be watched. If he leaves the state he'll be yanked back, put behind bars, his bail revoked. And you'll be safe.''

She swallowed. "Will I?''

He hadn't meant to stand so close, to touch her. It messed with his thinking, gave him ideas he knew were wrong...but he couldn't bring himself to step back. "I'm not going to let him hurt you, Emma.''

Her tongue moistened her lips. Her gaze remained steady on his. "Am I safe with you? Are you...are you going to kiss me?''

"No! No, I said I wouldn't...'' But his mouth was hovering a breath away from hers. His hand was on her face, tilting it up toward his. He rubbed her jaw with his thumb. "I shouldn't.''

"I need to tell you something.''

"All right.'' The soft skin under her jaw captivated him. He stroked his fingertips along it.

"It's important.''

"Okay.'' He was in control, he assured himself. He wouldn't kiss her. But touching her here, where the pulse beat so quickly in her throat, felt so good. And here, along the slope of her shoulder, where the fabric of her dress met the warmth of her flesh, then dipped toward the swell of her breasts....

"You think I'm looking for something permanent, and I'm not.''

His head jerked back.

"I should be.'' Her sigh was so soft he barely heard it. "I do want the kind of forever-after that some people find, but we can't always have what we want, can we? I'm not a forever kind of woman, Flynn. There's something missing in me. I never can seem to...I wish you wouldn't look at me that way.''

"Are you saying you want a fling?'' he growled. "A

short, hot affair? Or maybe just a quickie to settle those hormones of yours?''

''Isn't that the only sort of relationship you're interested in? Something pleasant and temporary. No strings.''

Yes. And it infuriated him for her to say she wanted the same thing. ''Is this what you want, then?'' And he crushed his mouth down on hers.

This was no sweet kiss, no gentle wooing. This was speed. Fire. Need. Emma's hands went limp in shock. And between one blink of the eye and the next, her world turned over.

Heat poured through her, a rush too keen and edgy to be called pleasure. Flynn's mouth tasted of coffee and the wild, burned flavor the air holds a second after lightning strikes. His hands imprisoned her face and his tongue plunged inside.

Never, never had a man kissed her like this, with a need so complete, so desperately carnal. His hand shifted to her hips, pulling her against him, but it wasn't enough. She couldn't get close enough with her belly between them. Her breasts ached for the pressure she couldn't find, no matter how she shifted against him. Then his hand came up to cover one breast.

She moaned into his mouth. He made a low sound of approval. Hunger fisted in her middle, making her head swim and her hands hasty to touch, to explore. He felt so good to her, so right.

The baby chose that moment to turn a cartwheel, kicking out strongly.

Flynn froze.

Emma's eyes drifted open. He looked so funny, his wide eyes brimming with startlement and alarm. His expression brought a flood of tenderness to mix with the heat.

His hand slid from her breast to her belly. The baby rewarded his curiosity with another firm kick.

It was delight she saw spread over his face now, delight and wonder. He stretched his hand wider, as if he were trying to hold the baby.

Somewhere deep inside, Emma felt a gentle motion like a sigh, like the quiet parting of a woman's legs to receive a lover. An opening, as if a hand that had been fisted forever suddenly relaxed. The sensation so small and simple she might not have noticed it…if it hadn't also been utterly new.

Her eyes rounded. She opened her mouth to speak, without the least idea of what she would say. And a raindrop fell right into her open mouth. Startled, she tipped her head back, and another one splatted on her cheekbone.

Laughter hit her with the same giddy delight as the feel of the baby moving had hit Flynn. Obviously she had no sense. She had no desire whatsoever to come in out of the rain.

Flynn tangled his fingers in the hair at her nape. His voice was husky. "The sky's about to dump on us. We'd better go in."

"Yes." In a minute. Or several.

"We could go home now. To my cabin."

She leaned back so she could see his face, hunting for meaning in his eyes. And there she found it, a blaze of need that announced that he didn't just want to return to his cabin. He wanted her in his bed. Now. Tonight. And oh, how she wanted to say yes—but was it right, for him? She reached up to touch his cheek, fighting for the strength to do the right thing in spite of the voice deep inside that whispered this was right. *He* was right.

Martin's voice startled her into jumping. "Sorry to interrupt, but a car just turned in at Flynn's place. You two might want to come inside while I check it out."

Eight

Flynn had a different opinion about who would check things out. Emma wasn't surprised by that, or that he ordered her to stay with Martin while he crossed the strip of woods between his cabin and Martin's. She didn't even object. She couldn't risk her baby. If it was Steven…

Emma shivered.

"Hope you didn't catch a chill." Martin shook his head reproachfully, but his eyes twinkled. "I'm not surprised that boy didn't want to come in when it started raining. Reckon he didn't notice, wrapped around you the way he was. But I thought you'd have better sense."

"I don't know where you got that idea," she said lightly, trying to ignore the hard knot of fear lodged beneath her breastbone. If Steven had found her, and if Flynn found Steven…the possibilities made her cold, deep inside. "I'm not exactly the poster girl for common sense."

"Nothing sensible about love," he agreed, reaching into

the closet near the door. "We're poorer without it, though."

Poorer, maybe, but Emma had been broke or close to it all her life. She was used to that. "Do you think Flynn— oh, God." Martin had taken a rifle from the closet. "I hate guns."

"Now, this is just a precaution. Chances are, whoever pulled up at Flynn's door is looking for directions, or needing to use the phone."

"Did you see the driver?"

"Afraid not. The trees are too thick."

"I don't know what to do." She looked around. There were still dishes on the table. She headed there and blindly started stacking them.

"You don't have to do a thing. Flynn will handle anything that needs handling."

"It's probably not Steven, anyway."

"Probably not. I—" His head swung towards the door.

A second late, Emma heard what had alerted him. Footsteps approaching. Whoever it was wasn't trying to be quiet, so it couldn't be Steven. It must be Flynn. She set the plates down so hastily they rattled, and hurried for the door.

"Stay back." Martin's bulk blocked her. "I'll just check…" He looked through the peephole. Then chuckled. "Well, how about that." He swung the door open wide.

This time he let Emma push past him. She set one foot on the front porch—and stopped dead.

Flynn was just stepping up on the porch. His expression was morose. And his arm was around the lanky, vivacious redhead chattering up at him, her face glowing.

Flynn's eyes met Emma's. His voice was resigned. "Be quiet for a minute, brat, so I can introduce you. Emma, this chatterbox is my sister, Carrie. She's going to stay with us tonight."

"For a few days," the little redhead corrected him, and darted forward to grab Emma's hand. "Emma, I'm so glad to meet you! I never get to meet any of Flynn's women—"

"She's a client, Carrie. I told you that."

"R-i-i-ight. Whatever you say. I—oh, Uncle Martin!" Carrie hurled herself into the older man's arms.

Twenty minutes later, the four of them were seated around Martin's kitchen table. Chocolate crumbs dotted the plate in front of Flynn's sister, who had managed to put away four brownies without ever quite relinquishing control of the conversation.

Carrie was an imp—charming, mercurial, obviously a stranger to the notion of thinking before acting. She didn't look much like Flynn. She was tall and skinny and moved as fast as she talked, and her features were more intriguing than pretty. She reminded Emma of a precocious child teetering on the edge of adulthood, blithely unaware that she hadn't yet truly plunged over that edge.

Carrie's conversational stew included frequent mentions of someone named Josh, who didn't appreciate her. Apparently the decision to visit her brother had hit the moment she finished the last of her finals. She'd driven to San Antonio, learned from his secretary that he was at the lake and kept driving. Her decision seemed based in equal parts on the mysterious Josh's behavior and on her newfound desire to go on the stage or to Hollywood—a goal that, for some reason, her mother failed to endorse. But the conversation slipped and slid all over the place, with dips into questions for Martin and Emma, and several quick digs about her brother's overbearing ways.

But Flynn was the one Carrie had run to when she had a problem. They were close. It was obvious in their easy verbal shorthand, the fast and friendly sparrings. Carrie touched Flynn often, leaning her head against his shoulder, pinching his middle to "see how many of those brownies you ate,'' and accepted his muttered ''brat'' as the endearment it was. Emma couldn't help feeling a pang of envy.

''So when are you due?'' Carrie asked, squeezing Emma's hand. ''I adore babies. And no, I'm not pregnant,'' she said, rolling her eyes at her brother. ''I just needed to get away from Josh for awhile. Flynn is always worrying that I'm going to mess up and get pregnant,'' she confided to Emma, then bit her lip. ''Uh-oh. Maybe that wasn't the most tactful thing to say?''

Emma couldn't help smiling. ''It's all right.''

''Is it a boy or a girl?''

''I won't let them tell me. It drives everyone crazy, but I want to be surprised. Like not peeking at Christmas presents before the big day.''

''You've got more self-control than I do, then. I always peeked. Flynn, do you remember the time…''

The conversation detoured into friendly bickering over Carrie's irrepressible curiosity. Emma stopped listening. She had to recover her balance. Her emotions had been on a roller coaster tonight. If Carrie hadn't shown up, Emma might well have ended the evening in Flynn's bed.

Flynn's eyes lifted to meet hers over his sister's head. For a moment his face cleared of all expression—except for his eyes. There, she saw heat. Longing. A mirror of her own, bone-deep confusion.

Emma sat bolt upright in bed, the sick miasma of terror following her out of sleep. She stared blindly at the darkness, her heart pounding.

A nightmare, that's all. Horrible, yes, and with too much that was memory mixed with the fearful proddings of imagination, but still just a bad dream. Steven wasn't here, ready to grab her. He was in California.

For now.

Her hand shook as she shoved the hair back from her

face. No way was she going back to sleep. Milk, she
thought, climbing out of bed. She would try that age-old
remedy for sleeplessness. But when she eased open her
door, she grimaced. She'd forgotten. Flynn had given his
bedroom to his sister. He was stretched out on the couch,
sound asleep.

The storm must have moved off while she slept. Moonlight flooded the room, giving her a clear, colorless view
of the sleeping man. He lay on his back, one arm flung
over his head, the other resting at his waist where the blanket was bunched. He was bare from the waist up, a statue
etched by moonlight and shadows.

He had an amazing chest. Incredible shoulders, too....
She shook her head. Enough. It didn't look like she'd be
getting any milk. The light from the refrigerator might
wake him. Waking Flynn would be thoughtless, and possibly dangerous, given the uncertain state of her resolve.

But she couldn't face her bed yet. The dregs of the nightmare clung, spiderweb-sticky. Emma hovered in the doorway for a moment before the lure of the moonlight gave
her an idea.

Her shoes were by her bed. It took a minute to toe them
on. Her nightgown was thin white cotton, too flimsy and
revealing to wear outside. Emma grabbed the matching
robe from the foot of her bed, slipped it on, knotted the
ribbons at the neck and left her room. She crept quietly to
the glass doors that opened onto the back porch. In another
moment she was sliding one open.

"Sneaking out?" a deep voice said from behind her.

She spun around. Her hand went to her chest, where her
heart was doing flips. "Don't *do* that."

"Think of it as exercise. I just gave your heart a great
aerobic moment."

"I had something a little less alarming in mind. It's a
beautiful night."

He frowned. "You aren't going for a walk now."

"Why not?" She gestured behind her. "The moon is full. It's practically daylight out there."

He studied her face in silence. She wondered what he saw. His features were mostly in shadow, unreadable in the tricky play of moonlight. The silence dragged up emotions she wanted to escape. Fear. Longing. The nauseous dregs of her nightmare.

"You can't go by yourself," he said at last. "Wait while I get my shoes and a shirt."

She thought about ignoring his orders, but knew he'd just catch up with her. And part of her wanted company. Some nights were harder than others to spend alone.

When he rejoined her, she headed outside in a silence that, this time, felt comfortable.

The moon hung directly overhead, so full it made her think of her own belly, all ripe and round. The world was moonsilver and darkness, the grass colorless beneath their feet, the shadows dense beneath the trees. Emma headed for the grassy path that followed the shore of the lake, listening to the restless secrets the water murmured to itself.

The ground was damp, slippery in places from the recent rain. When Flynn took her arm she frowned, not sure she trusted herself to walk beside this man in moonlight with his hand warm and inviting on her bare skin. "I'm okay."

"Your center of balance isn't what you're used to."

He was right about that. She felt deliciously, terrifyingly off-balance tonight. "I'm quite surefooted," she assured both of them. "I don't—oh!"

A pale shape moved amid the shadows under the trees. Coming toward them. Quickly. Emma's hand flew to her throat, where her heart tried to lodge. A split-second later, a huge Labrador retriever, silvery gray in the moonlight, trotted out of the trees, tongue lolling, tail wagging.

The stuffing went out of her knees. Her laugh was unsteady, aimed at herself for being so ready to panic. "Where did you come from, big fellow?"

"He belongs to the people two lots down from Martin." Flynn held out a hand, and the Lab trotted up and sniffed it hopefully. "Wanders all over the place."

She introduced herself to the dog the same way Flynn had, letting him sniff her hand, then rubbed him firmly behind the ears. He leaned into the caress so eagerly she had to brace herself against his weight. "Friendly soul, isn't he?"

"Yeah." Flynn picked up a stick and tossed it. The big dog gave a happy yelp and launched himself after it. "Usually when you can't sleep it's because you have to head for the bathroom. What sent you outside tonight?"

"Oh...lots of things." She tilted her face up to the night, tasting the damp, fresh air. "Maybe it was the moonlight creeping in through the curtains, calling me to come dance with the fairies. There could be fairies here." There was magic enough.

"Or maybe it was a bad dream."

A shiver skittered up her spine. "Maybe."

"About Shaw?"

She didn't want to talk about it, didn't want to remember...yet she found herself answering. "I dreamt that he was hiding in the bathroom here at the cabin. He grabbed me, and..." She stopped as the nightmare images, the terror and pain, swirled up. With an effort, she managed a chuckle to mask her reaction. "Talk about a pregnant woman's nightmare—attacked in the bathroom, where we spend so much of our time."

His hand left her arm, but only so he could put his arm around her. "Your nightmare wasn't funny, Emma."

"No. But sometimes laughter is the only thing that helps. Flynn..." She took a deep breath, let it out slowly. "I'll press charges against Steven.'' The nightmare had convinced her. She couldn't live with the fear forever.

''You're doing the right thing.'' His voice was low and intense. ''I'll keep you safe, Emma.''

Her heart pounded. How safe did she want to be?

The Lab pushed between them, the stick in his mouth. Flynn tossed it again and started walking, shortening his stride to fit hers. It was surprisingly easy to walk alongside him this way, her hip bumping his thigh gently with every step. He felt warm and real and safe.

''You and Carrie were doing plenty of giggling earlier,'' he said. ''I thought you'd never quit talking and go to bed.''

''Kept you up past your bedtime, did we?'' Because he felt too good, too right, she eased away from the comfort of his body. He didn't protest, letting his arm fall to his side. ''I like your sister.''

''Everyone likes Carrie.'' It was a statement of fact, delivered morosely. ''I do, too, but she doesn't have a lick of sense. This idea of hers about going on the stage...'' He shook his head. ''A few months ago she was going to be an astronomer.''

''She's young.'' Younger than her years, in some ways. Carrie had been protected all her life, Emma thought, buffered by the love of her family. ''A lot younger than you are.''

''My mother died when I was little. I was twelve when Dad remarried and started making babies with Stella.''

''Was that hard to adjust to?''

''Hell, yes.'' His smile was tender and inward, though, not bitter. ''Those two brats wrapped me around their pudgy baby fingers as soon as they showed up. I never had a minute's peace after that.''

Emma did some mental math. Flynn's father had died when he was twenty, so his sisters would have been very young, maybe six and seven, when they were left without a father.

They'd had Flynn, though. "You helped raise your sisters, didn't you?"

"Stella did all the hard stuff. I was around to yell at them sometimes." He chuckled. "Not that I mean to understate my efforts. Compared to riding herd on those two, basic was a breeze."

He had spent so much of his life being responsible for others. Was that why he thought he wanted casual, no-strings relationships now? She'd never met anyone better able to make the sort of heart-deep commitment he claimed not to want, or more deserving of it. But maybe…maybe he was right. For now. Maybe he didn't need to find that kind of relationship right now.

Her heart began to pound with possibilities. "How in the world did you end up as a private investigator? You were in the army, then you were involved with your father's business—construction, I think you said?"

"Yeah…if I'd been able to actually build things, it would have been okay. I like working with my hands. But I had to be a manager, an executive." He grimaced. "I hated it."

"I'm trying to picture you wearing a suit and a hard hat and making deals." She shook her head. "The image won't quite come into focus. So how did that lead into being a P.I.?"

"It didn't, except that I headed up here as often as I could, and Martin was here. Once I was able to get a manager to handle the business for Stella, Martin conned me into trying police work for awhile." He grinned. "I hated that, too. Not the work itself, but I'm not much of a team player."

"A lone wolf, huh?"

"Just plain ornery, according to Martin. I like to do

things my way.'' He took her hand, swinging it casually between them as they ambled along.

Emma couldn't take his touch casually. Though the connection itself was seductively simple, the heat that filled her wasn't. She felt as if she held a ball of light where their palms joined. It gathered slowly as they walked on without speaking, the easy lapping of the water the only sound.

His thumb rubbed across her palm. Again the gesture seemed casual. Again it was seductive, that slowly stroking thumb.

Was he doing this on purpose?

Did she care?

''Flynn…'' She stopped and faced him, still holding his hand. And got one, at least, of her questions answered. His touch was anything but casual. The dark look in his eyes, the pleasure spreading across his face when he saw her expression, told her that. ''Your sister's back at the cabin,'' she said, breathless.

''But we aren't.'' He stroked her palm again. Slowly and oh, so deliberately. ''Want to make out?''

A laugh caught in her throat. Make out? It sounded silly and sweet and spicy all at once. Innocence flirting with the forbidden. She pulled her hand away from his so she could rest it on his chest. ''Have you changed your mind, then?''

''No, I…'' He made a frustrated sound and shoved a hand through his hair. That errant curl fell right back down on his forehead again. ''You're right. I shouldn't…what happens between us when I touch you is too powerful to be played with.''

''That's not what I meant.'' She laid her other hand on his chest and looked at him squarely. The silvery light left his eyes shadowed. ''Until now, I've been afraid for myself. Afraid for my baby. But my dream—the nightmare that sent me out of my room—''

"Don't." He laid a hand over one of hers. "Don't call it up again."

"You were in it, too. And he—he killed you." The jolt of terror and grief hit her again. And the shame. "I just stood there. You know how you freeze in dreams sometimes? I was screaming inside my head, but I couldn't make a sound, couldn't lift my hand or take a step, because I was terrified. You lay there at my feet, all bloody and not moving. And it was my fault. All my fault."

"Shh." He put his hands on her shoulders and kneaded gently. "I know you think Shaw is some kind of mastermind, but I'm pretty good, myself."

Her fingers curled into his shirt. "It just hit me. All at once it hit me that I'm afraid for you, too, and that's exhausting, Flynn. Being so scared for you, too."

"Don't be." And his head came down, swiftly, surely, so that his mouth covered hers.

Relief. It poured through her, thick and drugging. His taste, the pressure of his mouth, was sheer relief, blotting out fear and erasing thought. His skin was cool from the night air. His lips were warm. She cradled his cheek in one hand, testing the roughness, the beard-bristles. Tomorrow seemed impossibly distant.

Their mouths opened at the same instant. His tongue came courting, slippery-rough, and hers joined the dance to build a tangled flavor that was part him, part her. There were tastes here that needed to be freed—a hint of toothpaste, a whisper of copper from the blood coursing beneath his skin. And the ripe, dark, red flavor of hunger.

He made a sound low in his throat and gathered her closer. The thin cotton of her gown and robe felt like no barrier at all, and when his hand found a path to her breast, his palm was deliciously warm. She murmured wordless approval, pressing against him. Along the curve of her belly, his arousal jumped in response.

As quickly as that, pleasure spiked into need. And fear.

No. No, she wouldn't give in to the fear. It had no place here, with the two of them. Emma went up on tiptoe, pressing herself along him, needing to feel him with every inch of her. It wasn't enough. His arms tightened around her even more, so that the buttons on his shirt dug into her breasts. His mouth turned avid, eating at hers with a force that made her skin prickle and her thighs quiver. For him.

Not enough. His clothes were in the way. So were hers. Desire danced over her, a mad fire that sent her hand to the buttons on his shirt. She fumbled, but got the first two undone and found his chest, that smooth, muscular work of living art. His heart thudded crazily against her palm.

Not enough. She moaned in frustration.

"Emma." His voice was hoarse, his mouth pressed to her throat. "Emma, I…" Then he jerked upright, robbing her of his mouth, and pressed her head to his shoulder. His breathing was ragged. "I got carried away. I didn't mean…give me a minute. I'll be okay in a minute."

He was stopping? Stopping, when she ached so badly she was dizzy with it? Stopping, when she'd almost managed to outrace the fear? "Flynn," she said, her voice breaking, "I *want* you."

A tremor went through his big body. "Emma," he said again, as if that was all he could think of to say. Then his hand slid down her hip. And began bunching up the flowing material of her nightgown and robe. Up past her thigh, the night air a shock of coolness on her exposed skin. Up, until his hand released the fabric to travel over the curve of one hip, along the juncture between hip and thigh, heading inward.

"Open for me," he said into her cheek as his mouth sought hers once more. "Open for me, sweet Emma. Let me make you feel good."

She clutched his shoulders, feeling as if she might tip over.

"Let me," he whispered. "I've got you."

Emma looked at his face, so close to hers, and saw a strong man. A stubborn, bossy man who would unflinchingly put himself between her and danger. She saw passion there, and a hunger to match her own.

More, she saw Flynn. And she wanted him. So she shifted her legs to let him touch where she needed to be touched...and he did.

A bolt of pure sensation shot up her spine. Delight shimmered down through her elbows and fingers, making the arches of her feet curve in delicious surprise. And his fingers moved.

He cradled her in his other arm and began kissing her again—beautiful, tender kisses. Hungry kisses. While his fingers stirred her and stirred her, and finally sent her flying.

Nine

Flynn couldn't have smiled to save his life. His whole body ached with frustration, the muscles so tight they hurt. One part of his body in particular was pounding to the beat of his pulse as if there were a bomb inside it, ticking down to an explosion that wasn't going to happen.

But satisfaction flowed as fiercely as arousal in his veins. Emma lay against his chest, her heart drumming as madly as his, her body dishrag-limp. She wasn't afraid now. She wasn't thinking about her nightmare or worrying about Shaw.

"Wow," she murmured thickly. "I'm noodled."

Apparently he could smile, after all. "Noodled?"

"You know—melted, wiped out, made mush of?" She patted his chest vaguely. "Boneless and brainless I may be, but…"

"But what?" He allowed himself to enjoy the texture of her hair, spilling free over her shoulders.

"I think you forgot something."

"Trust me, I didn't forget." He ran his hand down her back, hoping to soothe himself. "But this isn't the right time or place." And he wasn't the right man. Not for Emma. He shouldn't have touched her.

He couldn't have stopped himself from touching her.

She straightened, looped her arms around his neck, and smiled at him. "My brain cells are fried, so I'll admit I'm not thinking straight. And I'm not a conceited woman, so it would be easy for me to jump to the conclusion that you stopped because you don't want a woman whose tummy sticks out farther than her breasts—"

"You know better."

"Yes," she said. "I do." And ran her hand down between his legs, where the proof of her statement throbbed.

He jolted, involuntarily arching against her palm. "Careful." He took her hand and eased it away.

She aimed it an intrigued glance.

He groaned. Her interested attention was giving that most independent part of his body ideas. It jumped happily in the too-snug confines of his jeans. "Come on, sugar. We'd better get back to the cabin." Where at least one of them could get some sleep.

He pulled her against his side, and she fell into step with him. Her eyes were heavy-lidded. She looked like a woman who had been well-loved…and was ready for more.

She didn't speak, for which he was grateful. He and Emma seemed the only beings abroad in a night spangled with stars, enchanted by moonglow. The scents were rich— the fecund smell of damp earth, the complex perfume of the lake. And another perfume, faint and musky and wholly female, that came from the woman he held loosely in one arm.

Her scent was driving him mad.

So were her fingers. Her hand rode at his waist, but it

had somehow drifted up under his shirt so that her fingers could stir the flesh there in small, not-so-innocent circles.

She was vulnerable, he reminded himself. Doubly so. What had she said? No one had ever wanted to keep her. She needed a man who would stay, not one determined to leave. He'd warned her, but her condition made her emotional. She'd admitted that. And her nightmare had left her shaky tonight. When the neighbor's dog had surprised them, she'd nearly jumped out of her skin.

It could have been something other than a dog that surprised them. His mood turned grim as he acknowledged that. He hadn't been aware of his surroundings at all. Anyone could have come up on them without him noticing. Guilt rode him as strongly as arousal as they neared the cabin.

Inside was a bed. The covers would be already tossed back, rumpled and welcoming.

He couldn't think about that. "Sleepy?" he asked, hoping to distract himself.

"Nope. My system's still fizzing. Yours must be about to explode." Her smile was suggestive and slightly smug. "Your sister told me she once slept through a hurricane. I find that very reassuring at the moment."

He stumbled over smooth ground. "It doesn't matter, because..." How did a man tactfully tell a woman he wasn't going to go to bed with her when he'd had her bare to the waist a few minutes ago? It wasn't a question he'd ever had to consider before.

"Flynn," she said patiently, "you want me. I want you. Neither one of us is looking for anything permanent, right? I don't see a problem."

Neither did the part of his body that bobbed in emphatic agreement with her. "It's, uh, unethical for me to be personally involved with a client. And dangerous. I need to keep my head clear."

She lifted those curvy eyebrows. "And your head is clear now?"

Panic. It wasn't the reaction he usually felt when a woman he wanted made it clear she was his for the taking. He didn't know where the panic came from, what it meant, but it hit with the force of a gale wind.

He stopped just short of the steps onto the porch. "You say you aren't looking for anything permanent. I don't believe you."

"Am I lying to you, then? Trying to sucker you in, trap you in some way?"

He shook his head. "Not on purpose, maybe." It was time for truth, as blunt and hard-edged as he could make it. Time to send her running off to her bedroom—alone. "But if I take you to bed tonight, you're going to get hurt. Or are you going to pretend to either of us that you aren't already a little bit in love?"

Her eyes were wide and steady on his, their surfaces liquid in the moonlight. Yet beneath the surfaces, shadows shifted. Her voice, when she spoke, was soft and sad. "No, I won't pretend. I'm more than a little in love with you, Flynn Sinclair. And that may hurt me at some point. But it won't last, neither the hurt nor the fall."

Something bit, hard and deep. And drew blood. "What do you mean?"

She looked away. "There's something lacking in me. I fall in love easily, but it never lasts. You should know that about me. I—I don't want to hurt you, either."

Pride made him want to deny that she could. Honesty kept him silent.

"Well." She pulled away, fidgeting nervously with the ribbons on her robe. "Thank you for walking with me, and…and I'll see you in the morning, I guess."

She started up the steps. And that fast, that unreasonably, the panic was back. "Emma."

She paused. Turned to face him.

His mouth was dry. He wasn't sure, but he thought his hands might shake if he held them out. "I'd take the risk for myself. I don't want to risk you."

"I choose my own risks." She held out her hand.

His heart pounded loudly in his ears. For the life of him he didn't know if it was fear or desire making it beat so crazily.

He climbed the steps after her, and took her hand.

Emma's bedroom was dark, full of the secrets and silence of the night. Her heart danced with nerves and need as she stopped next to the bed and toed off her shoes before turning to the man she would lie with that night.

He didn't speak as he untied the ribbons to her robe and slipped it from her shoulders, didn't ask if she was sure this was what she wanted.

Thank God. She had no idea what she would have answered. How could she be so certain and yet so terrified?

Flynn took both her hands in his and lifted them, palm-up, to his lips. He kissed one, then the other. Need flowed in, sweet and languid, not erasing the fear but making it smaller, less important.

Then he bent to kiss her mouth, and made everything easy.

The lazy thrill of his mouth…oh, yes, that came easily. Reaching for him, holding him, was the easiest thing she'd ever done, if not the simplest. No, what spun through her as he sipped and licked and sucked at her lips wasn't simple. But it was right.

Moonlight slipped in through the parted curtains, cool and easy. Desire slid through her body, warm and equally easy. She smiled as she unbuttoned his shirt, then shoved it off his shoulders. She needed skin to touch, to taste. To explore. Excitement shivered over her as she learned him—

the shape of his bones, the movement of muscles beneath skin. The way his breath caught, and the feel of that small, enticing patch of hair at the center of his chest. She bent her head to taste what she touched.

His hands clenched hard on her hips. He shuddered, and she knew a thrill of feminine delight. He was so big, his physical power so much greater than hers...until she touched him.

Tonight, they shared power. Tonight, he was hers.

When she licked his nipple, he shuddered. His hand fisted in her hair, drawing her face to his for a hard kiss. "Take it easy, sugar. I'll be careful with you, I promise, but..." He nuzzled her neck. "It'll be easier to keep that promise if you quit playing the siren."

"Am I playing?" She slid her hands slowly down his chest to the waistband of his jeans, and flicked the snap open. "Then play with me."

His hands trembled when he eased her back onto the bed. When he started to slip her nightgown from her shoulders, though, nerves skittered up her spine and dampened her palms.

Naked was best for making love. But naked, lying on her back, she would look like a beached whale. Her hand caught his. Her tongue flicked out over suddenly dry lips. "Maybe we could leave it on?"

"Emma." He cupped her face in his hands. "Which part of yourself don't you trust me with? Can you possibly believe you are anything but beautiful to me?"

He made her *feel* beautiful. With the look in his eyes when he pulled her nightgown down. With his mouth as it glided over her skin from shoulder to breast, telling her wordlessly how lovely he found the curves of her flesh. With his hands, treasuring and teasing, warming her skin as they slid over it.

Pleasure sighed through her, rich and potent. Then his

lips found her breast, his tongue teased the peak, and pleasure spiked into something sharper, edgy and demanding.

Her breasts were tender these days. He seemed to know, for he was careful, just as he'd said he would be. They were also sensitive, and her body moved restlessly, seeking his. She hooked a leg around his and drew him closer. The feel of his denim jeans against her bareness was impossibly exciting. "Flynn." She slid her leg along his, drunk on the scent and feel of him. "You're wearing too many clothes."

"I want to make this last." He nipped her throat, then licked it to soothe the small sting. "I want you crazy."

"I'm getting there." Her breath caught when his fingers found a spot at the base of her spine that was exquisitely sensitive. "Fast. You're the one who's dawdling."

He pressed a kiss to her collarbone. "We've got all night. No need to hurry."

"Speak for yourself." She sat up, pushing him onto his back in the same motion. Her hands trembled when she unzipped his jeans…. "Oh, my."

He wasn't wearing briefs. And Flynn was a big man.

He lifted an eyebrow. "Yes?"

"I'm not sure how…I mean, it's a little different with me pregnant. Especially considering your, ah, dimensions."

"Don't worry." His grin was pure wickedness. "It's amazing, the things you can learn at your local library. I've studied up on this particular subject." Moving quickly, he shucked out of the jeans. Then he stretched out on top of her, skin to skin, propped on his elbows to keep his weight off her belly.

The position pressed him firmly between her legs. Her eyes widened as sensation built.

"Now," he said, capturing her face in his hands. "Now you get to feel a little of what I'm feeling." And he took his mouth on a journey of her body.

Had he said he wanted her crazy? Between one beat of

her heart and the next, he snapped her into a strange new world where sensation ruled. Her skin dampened. Her breath turned ragged, her hands desperate. Reality tightened down to scents, textures, the kinetic truth of straining muscles and pounding hearts. He took her to the edge and held her there, then eased her back, soothing with gentle hands.

Then sent her spinning once more, out where sense and madness mingled, and sanity splintered. Until at last, when she was wrapped in the moment as fully as she was in his arms, he eased inside.

And the world changed again.

He held himself up on arms that shook as he flexed his hips and moved inside her. Sweat gleamed on his chest. A drop ran from his temple down one taut, strained cheek. She pushed her hips up to meet him and gasped. Giving to him, she only gave back to herself, made herself desperate to give more. She lunged up and cupped his neck with one hand, pulling his face down so she could stop that drop of sweat with her tongue as it reached his jaw.

He shuddered. Caught her mouth in a hard kiss. And moved faster. Like a fist, desire clenched tighter and tighter—then flung her out into the void. His mouth muffled her cry—and a second later her mouth caught her name as it burst from him.

Her chest heaved. His did, too, pressing against her with every breath. Flynn had collapsed onto his side, pulling her to him as he did. They lay cupped together, wrecked, exhausted. And happy.

Like an old married couple, she thought. Like she belonged…in a way she never had before. And the first tendrils of alarm snaked in.

Not yet, she thought, drowsy and stubborn. She wouldn't think about what had happened, what had changed…yet.

It was late. No bands of silvery light slipped through the

crack in the curtains now, leaving darkness to lie heavily over the room. Maybe the moon had set, or a drift of clouds hid that round, white face. Outside, an owl hooted, its cry muted by walls and glass. Inside Emma's womb, the baby rolled over.

Flynn's arm lay over her side. His hand covered her breast. Her head was tucked into his shoulder, and her belly rested against his. She felt the soft pressure of his lips on her hair. "Looks like we woke Abby up."

"Or Andrew."

He shifted to lay his hand on her stomach. "I wasn't too rough, was I? I tried to be careful, but you felt so good, so…" He pressed another kiss to her hair, as if he could only say what he meant with touch. "Was I too rough?"

"You were perfect." And that, she thought, was the problem. He had been perfect. Not that Flynn lacked flaws, oh, no. He was stubborn, bossy, a little too full of himself…and *right*. Right for her in a way no one had ever been, right in a way that went beyond sense.

Emma swallowed the knot of panic that tried to lodge in her throat. "That reminds me. What did you mean about studying up at the library?"

"Did you know that Dr. Ruth coauthored a book on pregnancy?" He grinned. "I enjoyed her slant on the subject. It made a nice change from reading about preeclampsia and placental abruption."

"How many books did you read?"

"I skimmed some at the library, checked out a couple." His one-shoulder shrug dismissed the subject. "I didn't know anything about pregnancy. I needed to."

She was moved by his need to understand. He did care. "Did you check out Dr. Ruth's book?"

"You bet. Inspiring material." He touched his finger to the corner of her eye. "You're going to worry me if you start crying."

"You're lucky I'm only leaking a little, not sobbing." She dug deep inside for the strength to turn her smile teasing. "I warned you, but you went and overstimulated me anyway."

He ran a hand up her side to her breast, pausing there to give her nipple a quick, teasing brush. "I thought you were stimulated just about right." Then he sighed. "But you need your sleep. I'd better go."

It hurt. It hurt more than it should have, more than she could have guessed it would, that he didn't want to stay once they'd had sex. Still, she tried to keep things light. "Afraid I'll wake you up nine times before morning with my trips to the bathroom?"

"No, I'm afraid my little sister would jump to all sorts of conclusions if I were still in your bed in the morning." He brushed his lips over her cheek. "She'd make us both miserable, teasing about wedding bells. Thank God she's leaving tomorrow."

"Yes," she said as he climbed out of her bed and reached for his pants. "Thank goodness for that."

He didn't know. For awhile, as Emma lay alone and sleepless in the dark after Flynn left, that thought filled her mind, large and impossible to grasp. In spite of the darkness, in spite of her efforts to hide what she was feeling, she couldn't understand how he could fail to know. It had been in every touch, every word. In the way she'd cried out when they were joined, and in each breath she'd breathed against his skin afterwards.

How could he not have seen, touched, tasted her love?

It was best this way, she told herself. He'd believed her when she said she wasn't looking for tomorrows. He wouldn't have come to her bed otherwise.

At the time, she'd believed it herself.

She'd been an idiot. Blind, yes, but how could she blame herself for that? You couldn't explain red to a woman who had never seen colors before. She hadn't known. She'd simply had no clue what real love meant, how deeply it cut, making her want. And hurt. And hope. She'd thought she could choose to be reasonable, to accept what he offered and rejoice in what she could give him in return.

She hadn't known love was a thief. It robbed her of choices. She couldn't help longing for the tomorrows she'd told him she didn't need, but the timing was as wrong as the man was right. She was pregnant with another man's child.

Oh, Flynn was capable of loving and raising a child he hadn't fathered. Wasn't that what he'd done with his sisters? But his father's death had stolen his young man's freedom from him. The last thing he wanted was to find himself burdened with another ready-made family.

Maybe, she told herself, in a year or two he would begin to feel the need for more. For permanence.

Permanence? She grimaced. Who was she fooling? Maybe what she felt was different, but she still didn't know if *she* could be different. Until she did, she had to keep things light and friendly, just as he wanted.

Flynn wouldn't be hurt. That, she promised herself. She would give them both time—time for him to want what she wanted. Time for her to know if she could truly give him what she ached to give.

It wouldn't be easy. She was already hurting, and it was going to get worse before it got better…if it ever did.

Ten

___

Flynn sat on the dock sipping coffee and watching the sun smear color across the eastern sky. The water reflected the heavens so perfectly it seemed as if a slice of sky had slid to earth to rest at his feet.

Sky up, sky down, nothing but sky all around.

Hell. Now he was thinking in lines of bad verse. He shook his head. Sleep deprivation had obviously addled his brain. But what did a man do when he lost the ground beneath his feet to a tricky imitation of heaven?

She made him feel too much. It wasn't right, wasn't what he wanted...but he wanted her. Oh, yes, he wanted her— under him, moving with him, touching and caressing and opening to him. That, he could understand. But he also wanted her snuggled up to him in sleep. Smiling at him over morning coffee. He wanted to watch her twist her legs into pretzels while she chanted her *oms,* and hear her tease him about eating his veggies. He wanted to rub her back when it ached, and make her rest when she needed it.

He wanted, badly, to watch her child being born.

It was no consolation to learn that he'd been right all along. Emma wasn't a temporary kind of woman. She was the kind who burned her way into a man's soul and stayed there.

But she didn't want promises, didn't believe she was capable of hanging in there for the long haul. And she had a history of moving on, didn't she? How many towns and cities had she left behind since leaving her hometown? And she never looked back. She prided herself on that, on leaving the past in the dust, but it was a concept more foreign to Flynn than Chinese. The present didn't exist in a bubble by itself; it was built on the past.

Maybe a woman who'd never known what her father's face looked like couldn't afford the past. Maybe Emma wasn't capable of commitment. It was painfully possible. Look at the way she held her own mother at arm's length.

But she deserved the promises she didn't want. She needed someone who would stay, someone who would show her patiently that he could be counted on. Someone to believe in. Someone who wouldn't climb out of her bed so fast he practically left skid marks.

Flynn scrubbed his hand across his face. He'd dreamed of freedom for so long. If he gave it up for Emma and her child, would he end up resenting them both?

He didn't know what to do, whether to grab her and hang on in spite of his fears and hers, or run the other way as fast as he could.

He'd tried running, though, hadn't he? He'd practically thrown himself out of her bed last night in a blind panic. And then he'd run for real, pulling on his shoes and taking off down the road that rambled around the lake, hoping to burn some clarity into his brain.

It hadn't helped. Now he was tired and sore and cranky as well as confused.

Behind him, dirt crunched quietly beneath sneakers. He didn't turn away from his contemplation of the sunrise. He knew those light, hasty footsteps.

A moment later, his sister spoke. "You're up early."

"Unlike some people, I'm not in the habit of sleeping until noon."

"I can't sleep till noon very often these days. Nine o'clock class." She sighed regretfully. "Being an adult is a lot of trouble sometimes."

He smiled faintly. "Yeah. Sometimes it is."

Carrie lowered herself to sit beside him with a grace that still surprised him. In some corner of his mind, she was still the awkward colt of a girl who had watched him with such sad, solemn eyes when he came home for their father's funeral.

She was all but grown now—and still ninety-percent legs. Still prone to throw herself at life at a dead run. He felt oddly nostalgic for the gawky preteen. "What dragged you out of bed at dawn this morning?"

She shrugged, reached for his coffee and took a healthy sip. "Ahh. No one, but no one, makes coffee as good as yours. Which part of being all grown up has you looking so sad?"

"I'm not sad."

"Churned up, unhappy, ready to chew nails and spit out thumbtacks—whatever you want to call it."

Carrie always knew. She might be more trouble than a hatful of fleas, but she had an uncanny gift for seeing inside people. It was damned annoying. "I'm fine. Can I have my coffee back?"

She handed the mug to him. "Something's bothering you. Or someone."

"We're not going to talk about me. We're going to talk about you, and this crazy idea of yours about running off to Hollywood."

"Emma persuaded me to stick it out at college another year."

"And how did she do that?"

"She pointed out that if I'm truly called to acting, I'll still feel the call a year from now. If that isn't my life path, it would be a shame to narrow my choices too soon. I can wait a year to find out." She smiled. "I like Emma."

"She likes you, too. God only knows why," he muttered, and made another effort to change the subject. "Listen, Carrie, if you want to change your major to film or theater or something, that's fine." Though the idea made acid churn in his stomach. The entertainment industry chewed up dreams and innocence with such indifferent relish. "But whatever direction you choose, finish your education."

"Education is never truly finished, though, is it? When did Emma tell you she liked me? You went to bed before Emma and I did last night."

"She woke up. We talked awhile." He waited grimly for the cross-examination.

Instead, she captured his mug for another sip, then handed it back. "You remember what you told me the Christmas I turned nine?"

"No." He remembered finding her sitting by the tree, though, very late one Christmas Eve a little over a year after their father's death. She'd been curled into herself, crying so hard her spine had jerked with the sobs. But it had been rage, not sorrow, that bowed her over—rage at God, at Flynn, their father. At all the changes that grief and loss had rammed down her throat.

Carrie smiled. "You told me some changes can be fought, some can't. And that we hurt ourselves when we fight too hard, too long, against the changes we can't do anything about."

She rose with that fluid motion he wasn't used to and

laid a hand on his shoulder. "Don't fight too hard or too long, okay?"

Wasn't that just like Carrie? He scowled at the water as her quick footsteps faded behind him. She'd tossed him back his own words as if they held some great wisdom. But they didn't apply. He wasn't fighting some change that had already happened. He had choices. He could choose to change his life—or not.

He was confused, yeah. But that's because he wasn't sure of his goal. There was a huge difference between setting a goal and struggling against what was already true.

Disgusted, Flynn swallowed the last of his coffee, stood and started for the cabin. He was halfway there when Emma came out onto the porch. She wore shorts and a T-shirt the color of the sky in the west. Her hair curled frantically around her face, as if it had only this one moment to get all its curling done for the day.

His feet stopped moving.

She didn't see him. It might have been a trick of the light, or maybe her attention was focused inward. Whatever the reason, she didn't see him standing halfway up the slight slope of the hill, while he could see her clearly. There were tired smudges beneath her eyes. And she was glowing.

He could hear her, too. Flynn smiled. It was the middle of May, and Emma was humming "Deck the Halls" as she settled into her meditation position on the floor of the porch. Around him, birds woke the morning with their songs. Sunshine streaked through the trees to his right, falling in random beauty on the dirt and leaves beneath. The top of his head grew warm from the sun as he stood there, unmoving, listening to Emma hum a Christmas carol, her face peaceful, her hair frantically busy.

And quietly, peacefully, understanding grew inside him, as inevitable as morning.

He did have choices. Decisions lay in front of him, but

they weren't the ones he'd been struggling with. He didn't need to figure out whether he was running or hanging on with everything inside him.

Because he knew now. He was in love with Emma. And that changed everything.

In spite of Flynn's efforts, it was noon before Carrie left. Emma didn't mind. She enjoyed watching the two of them, and she liked Carrie a lot.

"You've got your cell phone?" Flynn asked, leaning in the car's window to search the cluttered front seat.

"I've got it." Carrie rolled her eyes over his head at Emma, who grinned back. "It's plugged in, too."

"Good. Call as soon as you get in."

"Flynn, I'm nineteen, not nine."

"Call," he repeated. "And fill up in Marble Falls. You don't want to run out of gas on the highway. You might have them check the pressure in the left rear tire, too. It looks—"

Carrie snagged his neck with one hand, pulled his head down, and gave him a smacking kiss. "Goodbye, Flynn. I'll call when I get home."

Emma smiled as she watched the two of them. Smiled, and ached.

Flynn thought he wanted freedom. Shoot, the silly man thought he *was* free. He had no idea what it was like to be truly free of all ties and responsibilities. Free of having anyone, anywhere, to love and fret over, who loved and fretted over you. He didn't know how loneliness could rise up to choke you in the middle of the night, how all that freedom could become a weight crushing the breath right out of you.

Emma knew. She rubbed her stomach with one hand and waved with the other as Carrie pulled away.

Before his sister's car was out of sight, Flynn turned to

Emma. His eyes were a brighter green than the grass around them. He grabbed her and made a funny, growling sound as he nuzzled her neck. "I thought she'd never leave."

She looped her arms around his shoulders and leaned back, feeling safe and cozy with his arms to support her. "Flynn, you're crazy about your sister."

"Yeah. So?" He nibbled at her ear. "I couldn't do this when she was around. And all morning, I've wanted to. This, too." He cupped her breast and lifted, squeezed.

The sun fell warm and sweet on her head. Another sweetness ran inside her, swimming in her veins and making her feel young and silly. She wanted to burst into song like the birds, or spread herself along the ground like the sunshine. "Do you always get amorous in the out-of-doors?"

"It's all the fresh air." He touched his lips to hers once. Again. "Makes a man lively."

"I like you lively." She gave him a quick kiss to emphasize that. His taste was too inviting for such a hasty sampling, though, so she went back for more.

He seemed to think that was a good idea—until he put his hands on her shoulders and eased her back. "Damn. Hold that thought, sugar. We've got company."

Alarm jolted up her spine, but she relaxed immediately. The company bumping up the long drive towards them was only a delivery truck. "I haven't ordered anything."

"Neither have I, but I think your mom did. Maude mentioned that she was forwarding something from Miranda."

"Oh." She fought the quick, instinctive flare of dislike. "She didn't mention it last time I called her. I hope it's nothing expensive. She keeps giving me all these expensive presents. It makes me uncomfortable."

"Because of the cost? Or because they represent something you aren't ready to accept?"

"Don't analyze me," she muttered, moving forward as the delivery van came to a halt.

The package was from Miranda, and it was expensive.

Also exquisite. Emma ran her hand along the crib-size quilt. The colors were gentle yet vivid, the material whisper-soft, and each quilted square was decorated with delicate embroidery. A bespectacled owl stared out at her from a dusky blue square that held a tiny crescent moon. A bright yellow sun smiled from a creamy square, while a trio of kittens curled up on the mint green square next to it.

"Have you ever seen anything so impractical?" she asked Flynn. The trace of wistfulness in her voice bothered her, so she started refolding the quilt. Out of sight, out of mind, she thought. "Not to mention expensive. It's hand-made."

"Is it?"

"Oh, yes. Just look at the embroidery…it would have to be dry-cleaned, you know." In spite of herself, a sigh slipped out. "Well, Miranda can afford to dry-clean baby things if she likes. I'll have to return it, of course." But her fingers lingered. It would be soft, so soft, against a baby's delicate skin.

"Why? It's obvious you love it."

"That isn't the point." Briskly she finished folding the quilt and put it back in its box. "I've asked her to stop buying me things. She doesn't listen."

"I could be wrong, but I don't think that's for you. Looks like it's for your baby. Her grandchild."

"My baby can use it when we visit. Miranda plans to have a nursery at her place."

"So you do plan to let her see her grandchild occasionally?"

His sarcasm sent hurt rippling through her. She fit the lid on the box carefully so she wouldn't have to look at what she couldn't keep. "What kind of person do you think I am? Of course she'll get to see the baby. I want my child to know her family."

"Miranda and the rest of the Fortunes are your family, too. And you're going to hurt her if you send that back."

"Don't meddle." She took a deep breath, trying to stay calm. It didn't help. "Dammit, Flynn, this is none of your business. I'm nice to her. I don't want to hurt her. But I have to handle this my way. I need time, that's all." Unexpected, unwanted, panic fluttered up. "I just need time to adjust."

"How much is she going to have to pay before you figure the scales are balanced, and you can forgive her for leaving you?"

"You don't think much of me, do you?"

"You don't have the foggiest idea what I think of you. Emma." He came to her, put his hands on her shoulders. "Miranda has suffered enough for what she did. *She's* your mother, not some fuzzy, idealized picture you had as a kid. Accept it."

"Why are you pushing me about this?" In that second, all she wanted was to shove his hands off of her. To shove him away, turn and leave and just keep going. The gut-deep strength of her reaction scared her—and held her still.

Damned if she was going to give in to it.

"I'm not sure. But it's important." His fingers were gentle on her shoulders, long, clever fingers that started to massage away the tension there. But his eyes were fierce and troubled, making her breath hitch.

Fear climbed her spine with clammy fingers, stealing the light from the day. *No one stays. No one ever stays...* Emma's fingers clenched on the cotton of Flynn's shirt. "Not now. I don't want to talk about this now." She thrust the fear down, way down, and smiled. "I'd rather get back to what we were doing when we were interrupted."

He thought about pressing her. She could see the decision flicker in his eyes before he smiled, too. "Okay. For now. Let's see if I can remember where we left off.'' He bent and skimmed her mouth with his.

''Mmm...that's close, but I think we were more like this.'' She slid her hands around his waist and snuggled closer, tilting her face up to his. Now was all she had, and she wouldn't let anything spoil it. Not even herself.

His arms tightened around her. His mouth came down harder on hers, his tongue thrusting into her mouth. She held on fiercely and gave herself up to the moment. And Flynn.

He had time. Flynn reminded himself of that ten days later as he dialed the agency in San Diego that was keeping an eye on Shaw, who was out on bail. Emma had filed the charges the day after Carrie left—the same day she'd sent the crib quilt back to Miranda. Three days later, the San Diego police had picked Shaw up. As expected, he hadn't stayed in jail long.

But he had been watched. Every day.

Flynn was sure Emma wouldn't send him away until the situation with Shaw was resolved. And dammit, she wouldn't send him away afterwards, either. His hand clenched on the little cellular phone. He wouldn't let her. ''Sinclair here. What have you got?''

He listened to the verbal report, but part of his attention stayed with her. Always. No matter where he was, what he was doing, part of him seemed to stay stuck on her. Right now she was in the kitchen, washing up the supper dishes because it had been his turn to cook. She was big on rules like that, ways to keep everything even, with neither of them doing more than their share. That worked out okay when it came to cooking and cleaning up. Flynn had had about enough of playing fair and divvying up the responsibilities in bed, too.

Every time, he thought savagely. Every time they made

love, she had to do her share, too. She wouldn't let him give to her the way he wanted to. The way he needed to. It was a matter of vulnerability, he knew. And trust. She was holding part of herself back.

That was going to stop. Tonight.

The investigator finished his report while Emma was drying the dishes. Flynn asked a couple of questions, but part of him was listening to Emma. She was singing along with the radio...something about highways and wide open spaces.

No more highways for her, he promised himself. She didn't know it yet, but her wandering days were over.

Dishes done, Emma wandered over to the east wall and stood in front of the tall windows there. Outside, the light was draining from the sky. She crossed her arms over the swell of her stomach and looked out at the smoke and shadows of twilight.

Tonight she wore a simple sundress in vivid blue. Her hair was gathered in a messy knot on top of her head. As he watched, her lips turned up at the corners and her expression turned inward. Like a cat, he thought, with her senses tuned to a reality only she was aware of. And, like a cat, she looked pretty smug about it.

He smiled as he put down the phone and crossed to her.

"Hi, there," she said when he came up behind her and circled her in his arms. "I noticed you managed to make your phone call last until the dishes were done."

"I'm no dummy." Flynn rubbed his cheek against the top of her head. He loved the way her hair felt against his skin.

"So." She kept her voice light, but he felt the tension in her. "What's the news?"

"Shaw is still holed up. Two of his friends have come to see him, but he hasn't taken a job, hasn't left his condo except for a late-night trip to the convenience store Wednesday.''

She was silent a moment. ''It makes me uneasy to think of him closed up in his place alone, brooding. He'll be planning how to get back at me.''

''Then don't think.'' He bent to nibble on her neck. The taste of her, the scent of her, filled him. ''We've got better things to do.''

The hitch in her breath pleased him. So did the look in her eyes when she turned in his arms to face him, her head tilted, mischief lighting her face while heat made her body loose and supple against his. ''Now, what could that be? The dishes are done.''

''I've probably got a deck of cards around here somewhere. We could play gin.'' Four big buttons held her dress up—one each at the shoulder straps, two more at the short bodice. He undid the one on her left shoulder.

The smile started in her eyes, slow and lazy. ''I don't think you'll find any cards where you're looking.''

''Just trying to make you more comfortable. Your skin is warm and damp. All that hot water made you sweaty.'' He toyed with the top button on the bodice, then slid it slowly out of its hole. ''There's always chess.''

''Chess?'' Her hand slid under his T-shirt. ''I didn't know you played.'' She feathered her fingernails across his stomach.

The muscles there contracted. Hard. ''I love to play.'' He undid the button on the other shoulder, and her dress slid partway down the curve of her breasts, only one button holding it up now. ''But we should cool you off first. You might have trouble concentrating on your moves...'' He bent and flicked his tongue across her collarbone. ''When you're so hot.''

When he scraped his teeth over the spot he'd licked, her breath sucked in. She retaliated by dropping her hand to

the waist of his jeans and toying with the snap. "So, what
are you suggesting?" Deftly she flicked the snap open.
"Nude chess?"

"Knight to castle two," he murmured, and unfastened
the last button, letting her dress spill to the floor at her feet.
Her breasts were creamy and full above the cups of her
bra—a thoroughly sensible cotton bra in an eye-popping
shade of fuschia. "Or maybe I mean capture two." His
hands did just that, covering her breasts.

He would make her forget, he vowed. For the rest of the
night, she wouldn't think about Shaw or her fears. She
wouldn't think about anything but him.

When he kneaded her breasts, her head fell back, her
eyes closing. Her hands rose to cover his, and a fierce ex-
ultation filled him. She responded to him so quickly, so
completely. "You like that?"

"Mmm…" Her eyelids lifted. "I've got another move
in mind. King and queen to bed two."

"The couch is closer." He took her hand and led her to
the couch.

She wanted him naked. He let her have her way, then he
finished undressing her and lifted her in his arms.

"Hey!" Her arms went around his neck. "You can't—
I'm too heavy!"

He kissed her to explain how silly she was, carried her
to the couch, and laid her down. In the deepening dusk,
yellow light from the lamp by the couch bathed her flesh
in warm hints and shadows. She was so beautiful. So ripe
and round and perfect. He looked at her and smoothed the
hair from her face, and his hand trembled. He would have
told her then what he felt, but the feeling was too huge and
liquid to be held in the dry cups of words. So he showed
her.

He dampened her breasts with his tongue and chased the
shivers he created from thigh to elbow to fingertips. His

need for her mounted, but he held back. More. He needed more…the taste of the skin behind her knee. Her low moan when he touched her and found her wet and ready. The way her breath caught when he kissed a trail up the inside of her thigh.

She pushed up on one elbow and threaded the fingers of one hand through his hair, stopping him. Her breath came fast, her eyes were wild—and still she tried to speak lightly. ''Enough dawdling. My turn.''

''We're not taking turns.'' He touched the tip of his tongue to the crease where her thigh joined her body. She jolted. ''This time, we're doing it my way.''

''Flynn?''

He heard the hint of panic in her voice. And ignored it. Ignored, too, the way her hand fisted in his hair, trying to force him back to her mouth. ''Trust me,'' he whispered, moving his mouth slowly up her body, pausing to outline her navel with his tongue.

''Trust me,'' he whispered again, pressing a kiss to the inside of her wrist. And then, his hands framing her face, his eyes fixed on hers in the gathering darkness, he said the rest of it. ''I love you.''

Her hands went lax, slipping from his back. And at last she gave him what he wanted. Stunned, complete surrender.

He kissed her gently, and slid inside. Her eyes were still round and startled when he began to move. Her hands fluttered over his back, restless, uncertain. He took them in his. He had the fleeting thought that if he could only go slow enough, maybe he could stay here forever, just like this, filling and refilling them both.

Night eased into the room with them, dark and supple and sweet. The air between them trembled with what they built, one slow stroke at a time. The edge, when it came, was a surprise. She quivered. He moaned. And watched her face as they spilled over the edge together.

Eleven

———

The sun was up when Emma stepped onto the back porch, but Flynn wasn't. He was still sprawled across the bed, sleeping as if he didn't have a care in the world.

That was good, she told herself. He needed the rest…and she needed some time alone to pull herself together.

The problem was, her brain wouldn't cooperate. She tried to meditate, but she couldn't empty her mind. *He* filled it. How could she focus on her breathing when every breath drew in the faint scent of him, still clinging to her skin? How could she relax when she could still hear him saying the words that had shattered her?

I love you.

Words she wanted to hear. Words she needed to hear. Words that made her want to sing and shout and hug the whole world…and lock herself in her room and not come out until sometime next year.

What was the matter with her?

Giving up on tranquility, she went into the kitchen to start breakfast. First she spilled the coffee grounds. Then she stubbed her toe on the table while carrying the eggs from the refrigerator—and the carton flew out of her hand and landed on the floor.

Emma stared at the slimy mess beginning to ooze out of the gray cardboard carton and started cursing.

"Are you sure you weren't in the army? You swear like a trooper." Flynn stood in the doorway, grinning.

She glared at him. "I dropped the eggs."

"So you did." He straightened and came into the room, grabbing the roll of paper towels. "Sit down. I'll get it."

She snatched the paper towels out of his hand. "I can clean up my own mess."

"Okay," he said, his amiability unimpaired. "I'll fix some toast and bacon, since we seem to be out of eggs."

She got the mess cleaned up. He got the bacon sizzling in the pan and popped the bread in the toaster. "You want to try your hand at fishing this morning?" he said between sips of coffee. "I promised to take you out on the lake, and the weather's clear."

"Sure." She tossed the used paper towels in the trash and glanced at him nervously. He was bound to refer to last night, and what he'd told her. She hadn't said anything then, and they'd fallen asleep afterward, wrapped close in each others' arms.... "You bait the hooks, though."

He shook his head slowly. "Nope. I'm an equal opportunity fishing instructor. No gender-based excuses allowed."

"I don't like worms." Why didn't he say something? If he cared how she felt, wouldn't he try to seduce her or impress her or persuade her? Instead, he was taking her fishing.

"We'll use minnows." He leaned against the counter, looking entirely pleased with himself and the world. He met her eyes and cocked one eyebrow quizzically. "Something wrong?"

She turned away and went to wash her hands. "I'm okay with touching minnows." Did he even remember saying he loved her? She sure couldn't tell by watching him this morning.

Maybe he'd already changed his mind.

"No?" He set his mug down and came up behind her, bending to kiss the nape of her neck. She jumped. He put his hands on her shoulders and began kneading. "A little time on the water will be good for you. You seem wound pretty tight this morning."

She slapped down the towel she'd been drying her hands with. "That's it. What's the matter with you?" She shoved him in the chest. "Why are you so blasted cheerful? Why aren't you asking me questions?"

His voice stayed level and calm. His eyes were anything but. "What kind of questions should I be asking?"

"I don't know." She looked around blindly, desperate for something to do, something to keep her hands busy. "Nothing. Never mind."

"What do you want me to ask you?"

It burst out. "Don't you care how I feel about you?"

"About as much as I care about taking my next breath."

"Oh, Flynn." She sighed and, as easy as that, went into his arms. His breath was warm on the top of her head. "I'm sorry. I'm so sorry. I'm an idiot this morning. I don't know what's wrong with me."

"Emma." His hand stroked her back slowly, down, then up. "I love you."

She shuddered. "I've been in love before."

His stroking hand paused. "I know."

"This is different. This—what I feel for you—it's everything." She swallowed hard. "I love you."

His arms tightened. "You don't have to sound so tragic about it."

"I'm scared."

"I noticed." He resumed the soothing back rub. "I'm going to marry you."

"Wh-what?" She jerked back. "What did you say?"

"I'd like to be married before the baby's born, but I don't want to rush you. You can decide on the date."

She pulled away with an uncertain laugh. "You're crazy, you know that?"

"Crazy in love with you," he agreed.

His eyes were so green, so soft and bright all at once. Tender. A trembling started deep inside. She began to pace. "You don't want any strings, remember?"

"I changed my mind."

"Just like that?" She threw up her arms. "You make all your decisions so cavalierly, do you? Just like that, you're ready for responsibilities, for a ready-made family…you haven't thought, Flynn. Me and my baby—we're a package deal."

"Damn right." For the first time a note of hardness entered his voice. "That part isn't negotiable, Emma. I want to adopt your baby, because it's going to be *our* baby. In every way."

She stopped, staring at him, perplexed. Her heart pounded. "Not in every way," she whispered. "It can't be."

"Every way that counts." He came to her, but didn't touch her. "It doesn't matter who started that baby growing in you, because he won't be the father. I want to be. Let me."

It was the hint of vulnerability in his eyes that undid her. Tears stung. She forced them back. "Starting a marriage with a new baby—that's hard. No real honeymoon, no time for just the two of us. You'd be so tied down, and it isn't even your baby.''

"Emma. Hush." He put his hands on her shoulders and shook her gently. "Lots of people get married, then end up starting a family sooner than they'd planned. And it *will* be my baby. I told you, that's not negotiable."

She reached up and traced his lips—so hard, unsmiling now. He meant it. He really wanted her—wanted both of them. "We haven't known each other long."

He smiled. Her fingertips still rested on his mouth, so she felt it as well as saw it. "How long did it take you to know you were in love with me?"

One quick bubble of happiness rose and popped out in a smile. "About a week."

"I was slow. It took me nine days."

More bubbles rose, giddy and delightful. "I'm still scared."

He went very still. "Do you mean yes? Yes, you'll marry me?"

"You never actually asked," she pointed out. Was that what she'd meant? Was she going to marry the man she loved? Her smile spread from her face to her belly and down to her toes. "Yes. Yes, I'll marry you."

He whooped, grabbed her right off her feet and spun her in a dizzy circle. She laughed and hung on. "You madman!"

"You can be scared." He gave her a quick, smacking kiss, then returned for a longer one. "That's okay. You aren't used to depending on anyone, but you can count on me, Emma." He held her close. "I'm staying."

No one stays. No one ever stays...

Emma's arms tightened around him. Flynn was different. She believed him, believed in him, and she wasn't going to let her fears come between them. "Have you ever changed a diaper?"

"Dozens. You ready to go play with some worms?"

"You said we'd use minnows."

"If I can change diapers, you can handle worms. Come on." He took her hand. "Trust me. It'll be fun."

She'd had fun. Despite the horrid faces she'd made when she picked up a worm, Flynn knew Emma had thoroughly enjoyed herself. She hadn't liked it when she realized he wore his gun beneath his khaki jacket. But with the will he'd seen her display before, she'd hadn't let that reminder interfere with her pleasure. He'd never forget her excitement when she caught her first fish—the laughter, or the streak of pure competitiveness that had surfaced.

"Mine's bigger," she said smugly as they climbed the steps to the back porch.

"Cussing this morning, locker room talk this afternoon." Flynn shook his head sadly, holding the door for her. "You've been hiding your flaws from me, Emma. Did I mention that the person who catches the biggest fish has to clean them?"

"Wait a minute. That wasn't part of our deal."

"It was in the fine print." He laid the stringer of fish in the sink and bent to give her a kiss.

She looped her arms around his neck and nuzzled his cheek. "Something's fishy around here." She sniffed. "I think it's you."

"Eau de catfish. You're wearing it, too." He was trying to decide if cleaning the fish could wait a few minutes— say, fifteen or twenty—when the doorbell rang.

She stiffened slightly. "I'll get it."

"No, you'll clean the fish." He gave her a last peck on the cheek and went to the door. The peephole revealed a young black man in a brown UPS uniform, so Flynn pulled his hand away from the butt of his gun before opening the door.

A moment later, he put a box on the kitchen table. "It's from your mother."

Emma turned from the cutting board, frowning. Her hands were shiny with fish scales. "You open it, okay? I'm slimy."

"Wash them," he suggested, but pulled his pocket knife out and slit the tape, then opened the box flaps. "It looks like more baby stuff, but…" his voice drifted off. It was a baby blanket, all right—an old, cheap, threadbare baby blanket.

His mouth tightened. He'd expected better of Miranda than this sort of cheap shot, which was obviously meant as a comment on Emma's refusal to accept her costlier presents.

"What is it?" Emma came over, drying her hands. "Oh." She looked puzzled and picked up the envelope that sat on top of the faded blanket.

There was a letter inside. As Emma read it, her eyes filled.

He'd never seen her cry. It made him helpless. "Sweetheart." He reached for her. "She didn't mean anything by it, it's just…dammit. Don't cry."

"It's mine." Emma lifted drenched, wondering eyes to his. "This was my blanket when I was a baby. She's kept it all this time…she says she's s-sorry it's so old and cheap, but she didn't have money for nice things for me when I was a baby. That's why she kept buying all those expensive presents for me and the baby—because she couldn't buy them f-for me when she had me." She burst into tears.

"Oh, Emma." He stroked her head, her back.

"She loved me." The words came out strangled between sobs. "She really did. She kept that old, ratty blanket all these years…do you have any idea how much I wanted something of mine to pass on to my baby? And there wasn't anything." Her hands clutched his shirt. "Now there is."

* * *

"Miranda?" Emma's lips curved shyly. She held the phone in both hands. "I just wanted to thank you for the baby blanket."

Flynn finished scaling the fish, and smiled. His shirt was still damp from her tears. Her face was a little splotchy from them, too, but there was a new softness to Emma as she spoke to her mother. She wasn't being kind now. She was reaching out.

He eavesdropped unabashedly while he filleted the fish. He was putting them in cool water to keep until lunch when she made a distressed sound. He turned to her. "What is it?"

She gestured for him to wait. "I'm so sorry...I suppose he was a difficult man, but if he hadn't hired Flynn, I would never have known about you and the others. Yes...just a minute, let me tell Flynn." She turned to him. "Lloyd Carter was killed in a bull-riding accident Sunday."

"Bull riding!" Flynn snorted. "At forty-nine years old? The idiot deserves what he got."

"Flynn!" Her eyes were large with reproach. "His funeral is today."

"Forget it. You're not going." He reached for the soap to clean the fishy smell from his hands.

"I think I should, though. He and I weren't related, but Miranda was married to him at one time, and he's—I mean, he was—Kane's and Gabrielle's father. Family should be together at times like this."

His chest tightened. It was the first time she'd claimed the Fortunes as her family. "Sugar, I wish you could go. But it isn't safe." He'd have to see if he could get someone with good eyes to keep track of who attended the funeral, though. If Shaw was as good as Emma kept insisting he was, he'd have someone there to see if she showed up.

"You're kidding! It said what? Wait, let me tell Flynn."

Emma turned to him. "Miranda got this letter yesterday—
someone is trying to blackmail her. She wanted me to know
in case whoever it is makes good on his threat."

He frowned. "Has she reported it to the police?"

She relayed the question but didn't get a satisfactory answer, judging by her expression. "We'll see about that.
When I come down for Lloyd's funeral…yes, but I want
to be there." She tilted her head, frowning as she listened
to her mother for the next couple of minutes.

"All right, all right. The two of you are ganging up on
me. I'll stay here so you won't worry." She made a face
at Flynn, listened some more, then directed her next words
to him. "Miranda says that Lloyd's wife, Leeza, seems to
be planning to stay in San Antonio. No one knows why,
exactly. It isn't like she has friends or family there."

He shrugged. That one would always have an angle. No
doubt she hoped to make some use of her distant connection with the Fortune family.

He was drying his hands when Emma surprised him
again.

"I have some news myself, of a happier sort," she told
her mother. "I'm getting married." She turned pink and
laughed. "Flynn, of course! No, he just asked me. We
haven't set a date, or decided on anything, really, except
that he—he says he wants to adopt the baby."

She'd told her mother they were getting married. She'd
wanted to share that. Flynn was grinning when Emma came
over to him and planted a kiss on his cheek, the phone still
held to her ear. "That's from Miranda."

She was grinning, too, but the joy faded as he watched,
replaced by puckered brows at something her mother said.
"No. No, that isn't necessary. I'm sure your lawyers will
have everything tied down properly, and even if they
didn't…I *know* this is a community property state." She
rolled her eyes at Flynn. "It doesn't matter. If you want

to…what?'' Every ounce of color drained from he face. She took an unsteady step back. "Dear God."

"Emma." Alarmed, he went to her. "What is it? What's wrong?"

She shook her head violently, but whether at him or at what she was hearing, he couldn't tell. "It's too much. I don't want it, do you hear? You can't do this to me!"

The money. Flynn's stomach dipped like a jerky elevator. Miranda must have told Emma just how rich she was going to be. He grimaced. He wasn't much happier about the thought of her upcoming wealth than she was, but they'd deal with it.

"Look—" Emma dragged a hand through her hair. Her face was still pale, making the temper-flags that bloomed on her cheeks stand out. "Look, I don't want to argue. Not now, not when we…" She swallowed. "I know, but you don't seem to understand…later," she said finally. "We'll talk later. I need some time."

Her eyes were dazed when she disconnected. "Ten million," she murmured. "Ten million dollars. God, I don't want it." She dragged her hand through her hair. "I'll refuse it. Or give it away."

In spite of himself, he was amused. "I doubt there's another woman in ten million who'd be upset at the idea of being rich."

She went still. "You knew."

"Not the exact figure, but yeah. I had a pretty good idea." He reached for her. "We'll work it out, sugar."

She was stiff beneath his hands. "You knew all along I wasn't getting any little trust fund."

A sliver of cold sliced in somewhere under his heart. "So?"

Her eyes were strange—dull, flat. "You kept saying you thought there'd be plenty left after I paid your bill." A sharp, wild laugh broke out, ending the second she pulled away. "I'm an idiot. God, you must have been laughing to think of what an idiot I am. Even when Miranda told me I needed a prenuptual agreement, I didn't—"

"Wait a minute. Wait one damned minute. You think I want your money?"

Her voice was even. Dead even. "It's quite a coincidence, isn't it? Last night you proposed to me. Today I find out I'm about to become very, very rich."

The pain hit in a split second, ripping him open. Almost as fast, fury followed—cold, freezing cold. Almost cold enough to numb the pain. "I knew you weren't big on trust, but I didn't realize how little you thought of me."

"Flynn…" She rubbed the back of her neck. "I'm sorry. I shouldn't have said that. But you never bothered to correct me. You knew I didn't have a clue how much money was involved. You let me go on comforting myself with my silly plans. What am I supposed to think?"

You're supposed to love me. The heart-cry went unspoken, smothered by the hard truth. What was love without trust? A wisp, a fog, an illusion built of needs and longing…. "You said once that when someone does something really wrong, an apology doesn't help."

She lost what little color she'd regained. And turned away. "Never mind, then. I can't unspeak my words." She headed for the back door.

"Where are you going?" he demanded.

"Walking." Her voice shook as she reached for the door. "Just walking."

The door closed behind her. He wasn't sure if it was guilt, pain or anger that made him let her go.

The sky was a bright, piercing blue. The grass was green and growing madly. She'd asked Flynn not to cut it, she remembered numbly. She liked the way it felt against her ankles, the way the wind painted ripples in it.

What had she done? Oh, God, what had she done? She'd had everything, everything she'd ever wanted, in her hands—and with a few words she'd thrown it away.

She'd doubted him. Oh, it had been horrible, the hollow, aching emptiness left behind when doubt drained the life from her. Doubting, she had hurt him.

The ground beneath the trees was dappled with sun and shade, but she didn't notice. All she could see was the stark hurt on Flynn's face when she accused him of marrying her for her money. And all she could hear was the cold way he'd refused to accept her apology.

He'd said he would stay, and she'd believed him. But he'd tossed her apology back in her face. And she…she'd walked away. She'd left him before he could leave her.

Emma's feet came to a halt. She hadn't tried to work things out, hadn't fought with him or explained or begged him to listen…but how could she explain what she didn't understand? Why had she been so ready to doubt, to accept the worst?

Because it had felt as if her fears had come true, instead of her dreams.

Emma's head tilted back, her eyes closing tight. The sun felt warm on her face. There was, she thought, a certain painful humor in realizing how much of a fool she could be.

All along she'd been afraid. All along she'd been sure, deep inside, that she would be hurt, that she wasn't good enough, smart enough, strong enough, to love and be loved. She'd been primed and ready for disaster, so ready she'd caused it herself. Then walked away.

Well, she couldn't unsay her words. That much of what she'd told him was true. But she didn't have to give up. If an apology wasn't good enough, she'd find out what was. Somehow she'd make things right again. He had said he would *stay,* damn him! He couldn't take that back just because she'd been an idiot.

The sound of someone moving through the undergrowth had her jolting, eyes popping open while her heart skidded into overdrive between one beat and the next. She looked around wildly...then laughed. It came out shaky.

"Oh, it's you." She held out a hand to the big Lab who stood nearby, his ears cocked curiously as he watched her. "That's the second time you've given me an aerobic moment." She smiled, thinking of Flynn saying the same thing.

And heard another sound, right behind her. Just before a hand slid over her mouth.

Flynn paced, cell phone in hand, as he waited for the San Diego P.I. to call back. He'd already called Kane, making sure Emma's brother would keep an eye out for anyone who didn't belong at the funeral.

He was being paranoid. He was sure of that. Shaw had been under constant surveillance since he got out on bail, watched by a pair of men who knew what they were doing. But Emma had told him over and over how good Shaw was. And she was out there alone. Because of him.

The P.I. watching Shaw's condo had thought Flynn was crazy to insist he make contact with his subject.

"He's already made you," Flynn had said flatly over the man's objections. "Shaw's a pro, and he's been under close surveillance for five days. No way has he failed to make you, so you won't be giving anything away. Just do it. I want to know beyond a shadow of a doubt that he's right where he's supposed to be."

Flynn's restlessness carried him to the back porch. He looked out at the lake, at the trees bordering his property. He couldn't see her.

Dammit, what was taking so long? He glanced at his

watch. Seventeen minutes. That was enough time for the operative to go up to the door, knock, confirm Shaw's presence and call Flynn back.

As if in answer to his thoughts, his phone rang. "What?" he barked. In the background he heard the wail of a siren or alarm.

"He wouldn't come to the door," a terse voice said. "It bugged me, didn't feel right, so I went in a window. Set off the alarm, I'm afraid." Flynn heard a deep, indrawn breath. "Shaw's gone. We've been watching his buddy, the one who came to see him two days ago. They switched on us, and we missed it."

Flynn was already out the door.

He'd seen which way she'd gone. North, towards Martin's place. Probably past it by now, he calculated as he moved swiftly among the trees. Maybe she was already headed back.

But his gut clenched with a certainty he wanted to deny. Shaw had been good enough to fool two experienced men. He had left San Diego two days ago. That was time, plenty of time, for him to be in place here. Waiting. Ready for the chance that Flynn had handed him to get Emma alone.

His gun was out as he forced himself to move slowly enough for silence. Surprise was too important an advantage to give up, no matter how the fear roared in his mind.

He had another advantage. He knew this land, knew where Shaw could hide—and how to come at those private spots without being seen himself.

Emma lay on her back on the damp earth. A rock dug into her left shoulder blade. Her arms were tied in front of her with a length of cotton clothesline. Another length of clothesline secured her ankles, while a third dug into her cheeks. It held the gag in place.

Steven had always hated dirt and untidiness. The handkerchief he'd stuffed in her mouth was clean. Her face was dirty, though, and damp with the tears she hadn't noticed shedding while she fought him—so briefly. So futilely.

He paced a few steps away from her, a golden man with dark eyes and a long knife in his hand. He hadn't hurt her...yet. Or spoken to her. He'd tied her and left her lying on the ground while he paced.

His silence was as terrifying as the quick, jerky way he moved. Steven was a graceful man...normally. Whatever surged through him so strongly he couldn't control it with his usual composure was far from normal.

But his expression looked normal—horribly, hatefully normal—when he stopped a few feet away and looked at her. "Why?" He asked that so softly, while the knife in his hand tapped out a nervous rhythm against his thigh. "I wish I could understand...pity I can't take the gag out so you can explain." The smile was sweet and sad. "That's what you'd like, of course. A chance to scream, to summon help."

He knelt beside her. "Sinclair won't come, you know." Casually he touched the point of the knife to a spot just under her chin. Fear razored through her, sharp as the blade. "He thinks I'm home, brooding over what you've done to me. He's provided me with the perfect alibi. When they find your body, the men he hired will swear I was in California all along."

She shuddered.

"Richard doesn't know what I'm up to, of course. You remember Richard Mathers, don't you?" The knife traced a light, stinging path down her throat. "He thinks I'm on a job. He's never liked you, but I don't think he'd have agreed to trade places with me so I could kill you. He wouldn't have the guts. Still, his cowardice has its advantages. He won't dare speak up afterward, either."

If only she could talk with him, reason with him, appeal

to whatever scraps of the man she'd known were trapped inside, lost in the rage and the madness. Emma made a small sound and begged him with her eyes.

He touched her cheek gently. "I wish this wasn't so hard. I hadn't expected it to be." He rose, the motion fluid. "I have to give Sinclair credit. I had the devil of a time finding you. I knew you were with him, of course. The two of you dropped out of sight at the same time. I tracked down his mother before I left California and called her. She confirmed that he was at 'the lake place'—inadvertently, of course. It took me awhile to find it, but once I knew which county it was in I only had to check the tax rolls. Are you sleeping with him?"

The question came too suddenly for her to hide her re-action.

"Damn you," he whispered—and drew back his foot and kicked her, hard. Brutally hard. Right in the belly.

Pain exploded, blacking out everything else for a second.

He turned away, smoothing his hair. His voice shook. "It shouldn't be this difficult. I know what I have to do. You betrayed me. I was supposed to come first. You knew what that meant to me, how much I needed to be first in someone's heart. But you placed a little clump of tissue and blood over me. How could you do that?" His voice rose. He stood there, his back to her, and he was shaking. "I loved you. How could you do that to me, Emma?"

He spun around and threw the knife.

It landed in the dirt by her head.

The strangled moan came from her. The bellow of rage didn't. A second later, Flynn's big body sailed right over Emma to thud into Steven.

The two men fell to the ground, rolling. Dirt and punches flew, but other than the sickening smack of fists against flesh, they fought in silence.

She tried to sit up. She might be tied, but the knife was

right beside her, buried in the dirt, and she had some vague idea of using it to free herself. But as soon as she started to sit, the pain hit again—a huge, sickening roll of pain that was nothing like the way she'd heard contractions described. She fell back, gasping.

Dampness seeped out under her. Oh, God. Had her water broken?

She blinked away the dizziness. Steven straddled Flynn. His hands were at Flynn's throat, choking. Then Flynn did something—a twist of his body that unseated Steven, some blurred-motion blow—and Steven's head snapped back. Another blow, and another. Emma needed desperately to see what was happening, but the huge, cramping pain hit and blurred her vision.

She couldn't be in labor. It was too early. It wasn't supposed to be like this, so sudden. The pains should be farther apart. She moaned and curled up around the pain, her eyes squeezing closed.

It was just starting to ebb when a hand touched her shoulder. She jerked, and would have screamed if she could.

"Emma. Emma, hold on, I'll have you free in a minute." Flynn bent over her, his face bloody and bruised, his hands fumbling with the rope that held the gag. She couldn't see Steven. "You're going to be all right, baby. You'll be fine."

The gag fell away. "Flynn, I—I think I'm in labor."

Beneath the blood and bruises, he went pale.

Twelve

The hospital lights were too bright. The bed was too narrow, the chair she sat in was as hard as a rock and the food was impossible. Not that Emma meant to complain, or sink into some sort of gruesome postpartum blues. She had a tremendous amount to be thankful for, she reminded herself as she let the magazine she'd been trying to read drop to the floor.

But she was leaving the hospital today. And her baby— her beautiful little Rose—was staying here.

Emma sighed and rose carefully to her feet. The stitches pulled, but it wasn't bad, just uncomfortable. And the tiredness was only temporary. Surgery was draining, even when everything went well.

And everything had gone extremely well, she assured herself as she wandered to the window to look out at the parking lot. She was a very lucky woman. Rose might have to stay in the preemie unit awhile, but the doctor said she was strong and healthy, and should be able to come home with Emma in a week or two. But it felt terribly melancholy to be leaving without her baby.

She stiffened as a car—a big, dark luxury car—pulled into the parking lot. Then blinked to keep the stupid tears from leaking out again, as they had all too often the last three days. Hormones, she told herself, sniffing. And post-surgical exhaustion.

The car was black, not dark blue. Not Flynn's car. Of course not, she thought, turning away from the window. He hadn't been to see her, not once, since she came out of surgery. Miranda said he'd been at the hospital every day. She'd seen him, talked to him. But he hadn't come to see Emma.

Obviously, the man knew how to hold a grudge. He might have saved her life, and her baby's, but he hadn't forgiven her for doubting him.

The door opened behind her. Her heart gave a quick, hopeful jump—then settled. "Hi."

"Looks like you're ready to blow this joint." Miranda came forward, smiling, to give Emma a hug.

Emma returned the hug. It felt good to hug her mother. Emma wasn't quite ready to name Miranda "mother" out loud, but in her mind she'd been getting used to the idea. There was a connection now, where there hadn't been before.

Miranda had been there. Every day, for the last three days, ever since Emma woke up from surgery, Miranda had been there. Emma was beginning to believe she wasn't going to go away.

"Where's Kane?" she asked. He'd been there, too, to visit. So had Uncle Ryan and Lily, and Gabrielle's family. And Justin. Her twin had flown down from Pittsburgh to see her and his new niece.

Everyone had come but Flynn. A cold, horrible knot tightened in Emma's chest.

"I asked him to let me do the honors." Miranda took Emma's hands. "I wanted to talk to you about something. Girl talk. He'd just be in the way."

It wouldn't be about the money, then. Which left only one likely topic. Emma turned away. "I wonder if the hospital has a dolly we can use to carry all of these flowers," she said lightly. "It looks like a florist shop in here, doesn't it? Everyone has been wonderful."

"Uh-uh. You're not getting out of it this time."

Emma flashed a look over her shoulder. "I don't know what you mean."

"Every time I've tried to talk to you about Flynn, you change the subject." She sighed. "Of course, he's just as bad. He wants to hear about you, but when I try to offer the teeniest bit of advice, he leaves the room."

Her heartbeat picked up. "He's here?"

She shook her head, her lovely blond hair swaying with the motion. "Not today. He's been here every other day, though. Hanging around the nursery, making silly faces at Rose. Pestering the nurses."

She shrugged as casually as she could. "He does care about Rose."

"Emma." Miranda's voice was exasperated. "The man's crazy in love with you. And eaten alive by guilt."

"Guilt?" Emma stared. "Why in the world would he feel guilty? I was the one who messed things up between us."

"Because in his mind, it's his fault Steven got to you. He thinks he all but put you in the hospital himself."

"But—that's crazy! He *saved* me!"

"I know that and you know that, but men don't have a lot of sense about some things. He blames himself for not protecting you better." Miranda turned away. Her hands fiddled nervously with the strap of her purse. "The one question I've expected you to ask, you haven't. About…your father.''

Emma's mouth went dry. "I…always thought you would tell me, eventually.''

"Perhaps…the thing is, Emma, I was a fool." The word came out harsh. "A far bigger fool than even a seventeen-year-old girl has a right to be, and because of my folly and my pride, you and your brother grew up without a father. And he—he never had a chance to know you, either." She turned slowly to face Emma. "Don't make the same mistake I did.''

"I don't want Rose to know Steven. Why would I? He's going to prison." Her voice shook. "I'm glad. I don't ever want him around Rose.''

"I'm not talking about Steven. I'm talking about the man who *wants* to be Rose's father. If you'll let him.''

Suddenly Emma needed to sit down. She backed up, finding the chair with the backs of her legs, and sank down onto it. "Flynn hasn't come," she whispered. "He doesn't want me anymore. I ruined everything. I've waited and waited, and he hasn't come.''

"If he won't come to you, you have to go to him." Miranda knelt in front of her and took her hand. "Or do you really want to spend the next fifty or sixty years wondering what would have happened if you'd tried a little harder? I can tell you from experience it isn't a happy way to live.''

"No. No, that isn't what I want at all." Slowly, she smiled. "I want Flynn.''

One week later

It was late when Flynn pulled into the parking space below his apartment. After being away so long, he had plenty of work to do, catching up.

He preferred it that way. Actually, he'd have liked to work all night, too, but his body insisted he sleep sometimes. And the chair in his office made a lousy bed.

She'd be in bed now, he thought. Upstairs in her mother's big, fancy house, sleeping. Miranda would take care of her, and she'd have plenty of help from the rest of the Fortunes. They were a close and loyal family. Emma and little Rose would be fine…no thanks to him.

Oh, God, he missed her.

Flynn's steps were slow and weary as he headed for the apartment he'd taken such pleasure in only a short time ago. Then, he'd reveled in being alone. Now it ate at him.

If only he hadn't started to plan, he thought as he fit the key in the lock. If he hadn't started picturing Emma in his living room, messing around with stir-fry in the kitchen or nursing the baby in a rocker by the window, it wouldn't be so hard now.

As soon as he swung the door open, he heard it—the thin, high cry of a newborn. God. His eyes closed as loss stabbed through him. He hadn't realized any of his neighbors had a baby, or that the walls were so thin. He'd have to move. He couldn't stand hearing that every day.

He gritted his teeth against the pain, stepped into the room. And stopped dead.

Emma sat in the rocker by the window. Holding Rose.

Flynn blinked. He'd lost it, truly and purely lost his mind.

His hallucination smiled shyly at him. "Surprise."

"Emma?" His voice shook.

"I'd hoped Rose would be asleep by now, but I'm afraid she's cranky. This is her first day home, and she isn't used to it yet."

"What are you doing here?"

She stood slowly, Rose cradled against her. The baby

stopped crying as soon as she stood. "Carrie helped me move in. Don't worry. She and Miranda wouldn't let me lift a thing except Rose—and they barely let me pick her up, either."

"But…why?" He ran a hand over his hair and moved into the room, closing the door. "After the way I screwed up…you don't trust me. You can't."

Her face was pale, her eyes huge and uncertain. Her hair was as messy as ever, but her stomach was flat now. And her jaw was set stubbornly. "I was wrong, horribly wrong, to doubt you. I hurt you, and I'm more sorry for it than I can say. I was just so used to shoving people away before they could…" She shook her head. "Never mind. I want another chance, Flynn. You owe me that. You said you wouldn't go away."

"Dammit, Emma, I nearly got you killed! You need a man you can trust, one who will always be there for you. I got involved with you when I was supposed to be protecting you, and it screwed up my thinking. I let you go out there, where Shaw found you—"

"I don't suppose it counts that you saved my life, and Rose's?" She crossed to him. "Flynn, you didn't screw up the day Steven found me. But you did screw up. Big time. When you decided to be noble and let me go without me having a damned thing to say about it!"

Rose started to cry again.

"You're shouting." He'd never heard her yell before. A smile was born somewhere deep inside, easing onto his face as warmth started seeping into all the places that had been so cold. "Yelling at me. I guess you're pretty mad." She trusted him. It was just dawning on him how much she trusted him. Enough to move in after he'd been a complete jerk. Enough to yell at him about it.

"Well, it was a damned stupid thing to do." Her voice

dropped, though, to a soothing murmur as she fussed with Rose. "There, there, sweetie. Your daddy is an idiot, but we love him anyway, don't we?"

Rose's daddy. Flynn's throat closed up completely. He had to swallow twice before he could speak. "Emma?"

She lifted her eyes to his, and now there was a smile in them.

"Welcome home."

A tremor went through her. Then she was laughing, and he was holding her with little Rose between them. And after an eternity of drought, he kissed her again, and tasted life. Warmth. Emma.

"It's good to be home," she said a moment later, resting her head on his shoulder. "At last."

*   *   *   *   *

More surprises are in store for
Justin Bond when he tries
to win back his estranged wife in

BABY OF FORTUNE,

coming only to Silhouette Desire
in August 2001.

And now, for a sneak preview,
please turn the page.

One

"**T**ake your hands off my wife."

Justin Bond stood on the spacious porch of the home he'd once shared with his wife and a flash of irritation whipped through him. He steeled himself to remain in control as he stared through the partially open door. He'd never expected to find Heather in the arms of another man.

Sucking in a hard breath, he balled his hands into fists at his side. His plans to woo his wife slammed into a brick wall. He'd come to ask her to give their marriage another try. It was a blow to his self-esteem to discover she was seeing someone else.

Reeling from the brutal tone of the warning, the man snapped his arms away from Heather, tripping over his own feet as he backed away. A nervous twitch appeared in his left eye. Justin considered that a victory of sorts.

"Justin!"

Shock and disbelief registered on his wife's face. She

pressed a hand to her chest, as if unable to catch her breath. Or was she embarrassed to be caught in a compromising situation? Justin wasn't sure which, and at the moment, he didn't exactly care. He wanted this jerk out of his house.

"Heather." Justin swiftly shifted his gaze in her direction again, and annoyance swept through him like a sandstorm in the desert. He clenched, then relaxed his hands again.

"What are you doing here?" She didn't wait for him to answer as she looked from Justin to the other man, then back at her husband. Soft pink color stained her cheeks and neck, disappeared beneath the vee of her cream-colored blouse. "Um, you remember…uh, Paul…Paul Dailey, a colleague of mine from school?" Her voice trembled slightly.

Justin acknowledged the introduction with a slight nod of his head. Twisting his lips, he studied his competitor. He'd always had that "slick salesman" look about him. Justin didn't trust him for a second.

"Paul stopped by to discuss some…committee decision we need to make."

Justin sent his wife a questioning glance. "Committee decisions?" His throat tightened as his gaze shifted with lightning speed to her companion. "Is that what you were *discussing* with my wife?" he asked pointedly. He put his hands on his hips, and it gave him a bit of pleasure to note a trace of fear in Dailey's eyes. "My wife is off limits to anyone but me. In the future, you'd be smart to remember that." The threat of Justin's words was reinforced by his grave tone. He heard the man's hurried footsteps, then a car door and finally a revving engine and squealing tires. If he wasn't so irritated with his wife, he might have been amused.

As it was, Justin stared at the woman he'd married, his heart slamming hard against the wall of his chest. Damn, just seeing her again after a year apart made his pulse race. Heather always had that effect on him. She was still as beautiful as the day he'd met her on the campus of Penn State during his last year of school.

Damn, a year was a long time without sex.

Apparently, it had been too long for Heather, also, he thought, outrage pulling at him.

"That was uncalled for," she stated, her voice sounding more stable as she began to absorb the shock of seeing him again.

"You're still my wife," Justin reminded her. "Apparently you've forgotten that."

"I haven't forgotten that we're still married." She faced him squarely, her shoulders visibly tightening. "But I easily could have. I haven't heard a word from you in a year." The reminder was spoken sharply, and hurt lingered in the shadows of her eyes. After she'd miscarried their baby, Justin had withdrawn from her. Eventually, their marriage had suffered irreversible damage, and he'd chosen to leave her. The pain of his rejection still had the power to make her heart ache.

Justin stated the obvious. "I'm here now. May I come in?"

"I don't think that's a good idea," she told him, then frantically glanced behind her and into the living room, praying that none of her baby's things were visible.

A flash of guilt swept through her. She'd never told him that when he'd walked away from her, he'd left her pregnant. He had no idea that he had a three-month-old son. Knowing Justin, if she'd told him he would have felt obligated to come back to her, and Heather hadn't wanted him on those terms. A child wasn't a good reason to keep a marriage together.

"I'd like to talk to you." Justin spoke with obvious control. Though he appeared calm, the underlying determination in his tone spoke volumes.

"Why are you here?"

Justin regarded her silently, then seemed to choose his words very carefully. "Actually, I want us to give our marriage another try, Heather."

FORTUNES OF TEXAS: THE LOST HEIRS
Fortune Family Tree

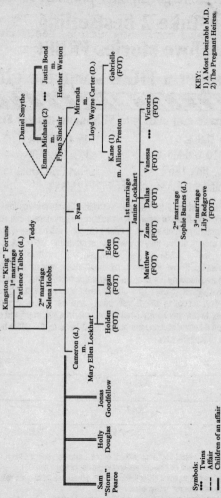

Symbols:

∗∗∗ Twins
—— Affair
- - - Children of an affair
m. Married
D. Divorced
d. Deceased
FOT Romance takes place in original
Fortunes of Texas 12 Book Continuity

KEY:
1) A Most Desirable M.D.
2) The Pregnant Heiress.

If you enjoyed what you just read,
then we've got an offer you can't resist!

Take 2 bestselling love stories FREE!

Plus get a FREE surprise gift!

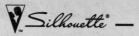

HARLEQUIN "SILHOUETTE MAKES YOU A STAR!" CONTEST 1308
OFFICIAL RULES
NO PURCHASE NECESSARY TO ENTER

1. To enter, follow directions published in the offer to which you are responding. Contest begins June 1, 2001, and ends on September 28, 2001. Entries must be postmarked by September 28, 2001, and received by October 5, 2001. Enter by hand-printing (or typing) on an 8 ½" x 11" piece of paper your name, address (including zip code), contest number/name and attaching a script containing 500 words or less, along with drawings, photographs or magazine cutouts, or combinations thereof (i.e., collage) on no larger than 9" x 12" piece of paper, describing how the Silhouette books make romance come alive for you. Mail via first-class mail to: Harlequin "Silhouette Makes You a Star!" Contest 1308, (in the U.S.) P.O. Box 9069, Buffalo, NY 14269-9069, (in Canada) P.O. Box 637, Fort Erie, Ontario, Canada L2A 5X3. Limit one entry per person, household or organization.

2. Contests will be judged by a panel of members of the Harlequin editorial, marketing and public relations staff. Fifty percent of criteria will be judged against script and fifty percent will be judged against drawing, photographs and/or magazine cutouts. Judging criteria will be based on the following:

    * Sincerity—25%
    * Originality and Creativity—50%
    * Emotionally Compelling—25%

    In the event of a tie, duplicate prizes will be awarded. Decisions of the judges are final.

3. All entries become the property of Torstar Corp. and may be used for future promotional purposes. Entries will not be returned. No responsibility is assumed for lost, late, illegible, incomplete, inaccurate, nondelivered or misdirected mail.

4. Contest open only to residents of the U.S. (except Puerto Rico) and Canada who are 18 years of age or older, and is void wherever prohibited by law; all applicable laws and regulations apply. Any litigation within the Province of Quebec respecting the conduct or organization of a publicity contest may be submitted to the Régie des alcools, des courses et des jeux for a ruling. Any litigation respecting the awarding of a prize may be submitted to the Régie des alcools, des courses et des jeux only for the purpose of helping the parties reach a settlement. Employees and immediate family members of Torstar Corp. and D. L. Blair, Inc., their affiliates, subsidiaries and all other agencies, entities and persons connected with the use, marketing or conduct of this contest are not eligible to enter. Taxes on prizes are the sole responsibility of the winner. Acceptance of any prize offered constitutes permission to use winner's name, photograph or other likeness for the purposes of advertising, trade and promotion on behalf of Torstar Corp., its affiliates and subsidiaries without further compensation to the winner, unless prohibited by law.

5. Winner will be determined no later than November 30, 2001, and will be notified by mail. Winner will be required to sign and return an Affidavit of Eligibility/Release of Liability/Publicity Release form within 15 days after winner notification. Noncompliance within that time period may result in disqualification and an alternative winner may be selected. All travelers must execute a Release of Liability prior to ticketing and must possess required travel documents (e.g., passport, photo ID) where applicable. Trip must be booked by December 31, 2001, and completed within one year of notification. No substitution of prize permitted by winner. Torstar Corp. and D. L. Blair, Inc., their parents, affiliates and subsidiaries are not responsible for errors in printing of contest, entries and/or game pieces. In the event of printing or other errors that may result in unintended prize values or duplication of prizes, all affected game pieces or entries shall be null and void. **Purchase or acceptance of a product offer does not improve your chances of winning.**

6. Prizes: (1) Grand Prize—A 2-night/3-day trip for two (2) to New York City, including round-trip coach air transportation nearest winner's home and hotel accommodations (double occupancy) at The Plaza Hotel, a glamorous afternoon makeover at a trendy New York spa, $1,000 in U.S. spending money and an opportunity to have a professional photo taken and appear in a Silhouette advertisement (approximate retail value: $7,000). (10) Ten Runner-Up Prizes of gift packages (retail value $50 ea.). Prizes consist of only those items listed as part of the prize. Limit one prize per person. Prize is valued in U.S. currency.

7. For the name of the winner (available after December 31, 2001) send a self-addressed, stamped envelope to: Harlequin "Silhouette Makes You a Star!" Contest 1197 Winners, P.O. Box 4200 Blair, NE 68009-4200 or you may access the www.eHarlequin.com Web site through February 28, 2002.

Contest sponsored by Torstar Corp., P.O Box 9042, Buffalo, NY 14269-9042.

SRMYAS2

COMING NEXT MONTH

#1381 HARD TO FORGET—Annette Broadrick
Man of the Month
Although Joe Sanchez hadn't seen Elena Moldonado in over ten years, he'd never forgotten his high school sweetheart. Now that Elena was back in town, Joe wanted her back in *his* arms. The stormy passion between them proved as wild as ever, but Joe would have to regain Elena's trust before he'd have a chance at the love of a lifetime.

#1382 A LOVING MAN—Cait London
Rose Granger didn't want to have a thing to do with worldly and sophisticated Stefan Donatien! She preferred her life just as it was, without the risk of heartbreak. Besides, what could the handsome Stefan possibly see in a simple small-town woman? But Stefan's tender seductions were irresistible, and Rose found herself wishing he would stay…forever.

#1383 HAVING HIS CHILD—Amy J. Fetzer
Wife, Inc./The Baby Bank
With no husband in sight and her biological clock ticking, Angela Justice figured the local sperm bank was the only way to make her dreams of having a baby come true. That was before Angela's best friend, Dr. Lucas Ryder, discovered her plans and decided to grant her wish—the old-fashioned way!

#1384 BABY OF FORTUNE—Shirley Rogers
Fortunes of Texas: The Lost Heirs
Upon discovering that he was an heir to the famed Fortune clan, Justin Bond resolved to give his marriage a second chance. His estranged wife, Heather, was more than willing to welcome Justin back into her life. But would Justin welcome Heather back into his heart when he learned the secret his wife had kept from him?

#1385 UNDERCOVER SULTAN—Alexandra Sellers
Sons of the Desert: The Sultans
When corporate spy Mariel de Vouvray was forced into an uneasy partnership with Sheikh Haroun al Jawadi, her powerful attraction to him didn't make things any easier! With every new adventure, Mariel fell further under the spell of her seductive sheikh, and soon she longed to make their partnership into something far more permanent.

#1386 BEAUTY IN HIS BEDROOM—Ashley Summers
Clint Whitfield came home after two years overseas and found feisty Regina Flynn living in his mansion. His first instinct was to throw the lovely strawberry blond intruder off his property—and out of his life. His second instinct was to let her stay—and to persuade the delectable Gina *into* his bedroom!

SDCNM0701